Jane Cave Winscom

Poems on Various Subjects, Entertaining, Elegiac and Religious

Jane Cave Winscom

Poems on Various Subjects, Entertaining, Elegiac and Religious

ISBN/EAN: 9783744716291

Printed in Europe, USA, Canada, Australia, Japan

Cover: Foto ©Andreas Hilbeck / pixelio.de

More available books at **www.hansebooks.com**

P O E M S

ON

VARIOUS SUBJECTS,

ENTERTAINING, ELEGIAC,

AND

RELIGIOUS.

By JANE CAVE.

WINCHESTER:

Printed for the Author, by J. SADLER,

M,DCC,LXXXIII.

To the SUBSCRIBERS.

YE gen'rous patrons of a female's muse,
  Ere you my works with studious eye
  peruse,
My pen would first in humble strains impart
The genuine dictates of a grateful heart :
Thanks to my friends—and should my labours
   please,
Crown'd are my wishes, and my heart's at ease;
My time improv'd, my musing hours well spent,
If these conspire to give my friends content :
But * Seward, Steele, or Moore, hope not to
  see,
With gentle candour read the Author's Plea.‡

 * Celebrated Poetesses.——‡ The first Poem.

THE
NAMES
OF THE
SUBSCRIBERS.

OXFORD.

A

REV. Mr. Alleyne
Rev. Mr. Agutter
Mr. Adams
  Annesley
  Amphlett
  Alexander
  Abbott
  Aldridge
  Apperley
Mrs. Atterbury
  Adee
  Austine
Miss Adams

B

Rev. Dr. Bathurst, Canon of
  Christ Church, 2 Cop.
Rev. Dr. Borrough
Rev. Mr. Bathurst, 3 Cop.
  Burton
  Barnard
  Buckland
  Bradly
  Barker
  Barrington
  Barnes

Rev. Mr. Booth
  Bond
  Beake
  Bright
Hon. Mr. Bingham
Mr. Cha. Burton
  Burgess
  Bell
  Batt
  Buller
  Budge
  Buckerfield
  Baillie
  Barton
  Brooke
  Beaver
  Blackmore
  James Brown
  Bracher
  Bosanquet
  Burn
  Buttlar
  Bull
  Brockman
  Bennett
  Batley
  Wm. Benson
  J. Bacon

1

Mr.

Mr. Blundell
Blackſtone, Queen's Coll.
Blackſtone, New Coll.
N. Barton
Barrett
Mrs. Brodrick
Borrows
Miſs Burton

C

Rev. Dr. Chapman, Preſident of Trinity Coll.
Rev. Dr. Cook
Rev. Mr. Cooke
Crowe
Coke
Clap
Collinſon
Hon. Mr. Cathcart
Tho. Caldecott, Eſq.
Mr. Crawfood
Coleman
Richard Cox
Chamberlayne
J. Copſon
Clavering
W. Carr
Coates
Chorley
Corniſh
Curtis
Cooke
Carey
Cowley
Calland
Caker
Cartwright
Commeline
Clarke
Compton
Challen

Mr. Courand
Clayton
Cobannel
Mrs. Caſtle
Couper

D

The Lady of the Rev. Dr. Dennis, Vice Chancellor of Oxford
The Lady of the Rev. Dr. Denniſon, Principal of Mag. Hall
Rev. Dr. Dixon, Principal of Edmond Hall
Rev. Mr. Davis, Bal. Col.
Davis, Mert. Coll.
Douglas
Mr. Drummad
Daintry
Dale
Donne
Deedes
Dardigareve
Dakin
T. Davis
Dallaway
Dornford
Davis
Davie
Devalangin
Davis, jun.
Mrs. Downes

E

Rev. Mr. Everleigh, Provoſt of Oriel Coll.
Rev. Mr. Edwards
Mr. Edmonſtone
Edwards, Ch. Ch.
Etton
Elliott
Edwards, Hert. Coll.
Mr.

Mr. Ebdell
    Edwards, Pem. Coll.
    Edwards, Jesus Coll.
    Eyton
    Eccles
    Ebdon
Mrs. Etty

F

Mr. Fletcher, Mayor
Rev. Dr. Fothergill, Provost
    of Queen's College, 2
    Copies
Rev. Mr. Fothergill
      James Fothergill
      Filks
      Finch
      Ford
Mr. Frankland
    Filmer
    Fhurlow
    Filmer, C. C. C.
    Fortescue
    J. Fisher
    Fernghough
    Flamank
Mrs. Fothergill
    Ford

G

Rev. Mr. Gould
      Griffith
      Godfrey
      Goutch
Mr. Gabell
    Gascoyne
    Grosvenor
    Gordon
    Greenhill
    Guard
    Gaitham
    Gray
    Gresley

Mr. Geary
    Gurdon
    Goode
    Gregory, Exeter Coll.
    Gore
    Griffith
    Glover
    Grubbe
    Gregory
Miss George
    Grant

H

Rev. Mr. Holland
      Hughes
      Heeghway
      Halfe
      Hayes
Mr. Harper, G. C.
    Harris
    Hyde
    Harrison
    N. Hill
    Hall
    Holner
    Hungerford
    Holyoake
    Tho. Honiatt
    Hopkins
    Hill
    Hurdis
    Hutton
    Howell
    Hooker
    Haskett
    Hulme
    Hurst
    Holt
    Hill
    Hawkins
    Hughes
    Hume, 2 Copies

Mr.

Mr. Headley
Hunt, Trin. Coll.
Harbin
Hunt, Pem. Coll.
Hereford
Hildyard
Hatton
J. Hutchinson
Mrs. Hornsby
Hawkins

J

Rev. Mr. Ingram
Joham
Jones
Johnes
Mr. Ilbent
Jones
Jeston
Ireland
Jones, jun.
Mrs. Jenner

K

Rev. Mr. Keeple
Knight
Kirrick
Knight, P. Coll.
Kilner
Kening

L

Hon. Mr. Legg
Hon. Mr. Littleton
Rev. Dr. Long
Rev. Mr. Lichfield, M. Coll.
Lichfield, W. Coll.
Lawthian
Landon
Lediard
Mr. Lee
Lindsay
Lockwood
Rob. Leigh

Mr. Le Messerier
Lysons
J. Langley
Leighton
Mrs. Lowny
Ludbey
Miss Lawrance

M

Rev. Dr. Mortimer, Rector
of Lincoln Coll.
Rev. Mr. Montagu
Moulding
Masson
Matthews
Massingberd
Mr. Martin
Meckham
Moss
Milner
Meakin
Milward
Mucklefton
Martin
Matthew
Mathew
Millward
Mead
Methold
Musgrove
Meredith
Marshall
Mrs. Morrell
Mayo

N

Hon. Frederick North
Rev. Dr. Nowell, Principal
of St. Mary's Hall
Rev. Mr. Newman
Tho. Newman
Nicholl
Mr. Newman

Mr.

Mr. E. Nares
Newman
Nash
Nettleship
G. Nicholas
Newton

O

Rev. Dr. Oglander, Warden of New College, 3 Copies
Mr. Oliver
Oldsworth
Ogle

P

Rev. Mr. Parr, Fel. of C. C.
Prosser
Pole
Mr. Peck
Prince
Pearson
Piddocke
Pulventoft
Payne
Parker
Percivall
Papillon
Plater
Paget
Phillips
Pasons
Phelps
Pitt
Pemberton
Powell
Parsons
Peachy
Patterson
Palmer
C. Plunknett
Paul
Mrs. T. Prickett

Miss Peck

R

The Rev. Dr. Randolph, Principal of Albion-Hall
The Lady of the Rev. Dr. Randolph, President of C. C.
Rev. Dr. Reading
Rev. Mr. Roberson
Routh
Radcliffe
Ruyeter
Rolls
Mrs. Rowney
Redwood
Mr. Rawley
Raddish
Roberson
Rouquet
Rupell
Ramnecy
Raisbeck

S

Rev. Mr. Smallwell, Canon of Christ Church, 2 Copies
Rev. Dr. Sheffield, Provost of Worcester Coll.
Rev. Mr. Sissmore
Stratford
Shaw
Smith
Spencer
Shore
Scott
Edwin Sandys, Esq.
Mr. Scott
Shutt
Smith
Stafford

Mr.

Mr. Smyth
Samuel
Spearing
Shawe
Stone
Sharp
Shaw
Smith
Shore
Saltren
Stevers
Slaney
Stuart
Mrs. Suger
E. Seely
Mifs Smith
Ann Smith
Sydenham

T

The Hon. and Rev. Dr.
Tracy, Warden of All
Souls, 3 Copies
Rev. Mr. Tanner
Tefh
Turner
Totham
Tahourden
Twopenny
Mr. Tomkins
Trollope
Tomkip
W. E. Taunton
Thomfon
Tyrwhitt
Trebeck
E. Tawney
Tomkins
Toke
Traleton
Trollepe
Tree

Turner
Trevelyan
Mrs. G. Treacher
Tucker, Q. Coll.
Tucker, Bal. Coll.
Mifs Taylor
Tuck

V

Rev. Dr. Vivian
Mr. Vigor
Ventnis
Vaffall
Vernon
Vaughan
Upton

W

Hon. Mr. Windfor
The Lady of the Rev. Dr.
Wetherell, Mafter of
Univer. Coll.
Dr. Wall
Rev. Mr. White
Wood
Warton
Watkins
Wifdome
Williams, W. C.
Williams, J. C.
Watfon
Welles
Woodroffe
Mr. Willes
Wingfield
W. Willes
Warren
White
Wrey
Wenman
Wroughton
Williams, M. Coll:
Wood

Mr.

Mr. Watter
Webbe
Wood
Worlcombe
Weſtern
Woodhann
Wood, Queen's Coll.

Y

Rev. Mr. Yeatman
Mr. Yates

WINCHESTER.

A

MR. Anderſon
   Mr. Applegarth
Mr. J. Auſtin
Miſs Anderſon

B

Rev. Mr. Ballard
   Bathurſt
R. Botten, Eſq.
Enſign Barlow
Mr. R. Barlow
Barker
Beckett
Brereton
Bowles
Burdon
Borman
Mrs. P. Bathurſt
Barlow
Berkenhout
Beckett
H. Blackſtone
Burgat
Bayſpoole
Biſhop
Miſs Barlow
M. Barlow
L. Barlow
C. Barlow

Miſs Blannerhaſs
Binghan

C

His Grace the Duke of
Chandos, 7 Copies
Her Grace the Duchefs of
Chandos, 7 Copies
Lady Charnock
Mr. T. Cooke
Cave
Carter
Curtes
Mrs. Clarke
Chiverton
Miſs Collings

D

John Dofwell, Eſq. Mayor
Hon, Mrs. Dormer
Mr. John Dowling
Dunn
Mrs. Dodſworth, 3 Copies
Durnford
Dofwell
Miſs Draper

E

Mr. Earle
Eaſt

G

Lord Gray
Rev. Mr. Gauntlett, 2 Cop.
Gabell
Geddard
C. Gauntlett, Eſq.
P. Gauntlett, Eſq.
Mrs. Gamon
Miſs Ginkins

H

Rev. Mr. Huntingford
Howley
Mr. Howley
Hutchinfon
       Mrs.

Mr. Harfield
   Hilman
   Hooper
Mrs. Hair
   Hide

J

Mr. Joules

K

F. C. Kirby, Efq. S. at Law
Mr. Kentifh
   C. Kirby
   W. Knapp
Mrs. Ker, 3 Copies
   Knott
   Kimber

L

Lady Caroline Leigh
Rev. Mr. Lowth, P. of W.
Dr. Littlehales
Mr. Lyford
   H. Lloyd
Mrs. Lee
   Leathes
   Lovegrove
   A. Line
Mifs Lee

M

Rev. Mr. Mence
Dr. Mackitrick
Thomas Middleton, Efq.
Mr. Milner
Mrs. Metham
   Morrifon
   Mofs
   Meader
   Moody
Mifs Mears

N

The Right Hon. Earl of
   Northington, 7 Copies
Rev. Mr. Newbolt

Rev. Mr. Norman
Mr. Newbolt

O

Admiral Sir Chaloner Ogle

P

Rev. Mr. Price
Mr. Parry
   W. A. Phelp
Mrs. Price
   Pawle
Mifs Pyott
   H. Pyott
   Parkhurft

R

Lady Rivers
Sir Richard Reynell
Rev. Mr. Richmond
John Richurft, Efq.
Mrs. Richards
   Rogers
   Raven

S

James Serle, Efq.
Mr. R. Serle
   T. Serle
   Serle
Mrs. Sturges
   Sparfhott
   Scoby
   Sadler
Mifs Sterek

T

Hon. Mr. Thynne
Rev. Mr. Tawney
Mr. Thomas
   W. Thomas

V

Mr. Vokes

W

Rev. Dr. Warton, M. of
   W. Coll.

Rev.

Rev. Mr. Williams
      Webb
Mr. Weſtlake
      W. Walldia
      Wetherell
      Wool
Mrs. Warton
Miſs Warton
      Wools
      Wheatly

Y

Rev. Mr. Yaldon
James Yaldon, Eſq.

SOUTHAMPTON.

A

WM. Andrews, Eſq.
      Miſs Alderſey
Miſs A. Alderſey

B

Mr. Brice
      W. Brackſtone
      Bernard, Surgeon
      L. Ballard
      W. Barnard
      T. Barnard
Mrs. Bridges
      Budd
Miſs Brice
      Binmore

C

Mr. Cropp
Mrs. Champion
      Cropp

D

Rev. Mr. O. Davies
P. De Carteret, Eſq.
Mr. W. Drake
Mrs. Daman
      Day

E

Mr. T. Evans
Mrs. Everitt
      J. E.

F

Dr. Frazer
Valentine Fitzhugh, Eſq.

G

Mr Grierſon
      Greenſtreet
Mrs. Greenſtreet

H

Lady Hughes
Rev. Mr. Halton
Mr. J. Hall
Mrs. Hague
      Howard
      Hoedly
      Hamond
      Hull
      Hookey

K

Rev. Mr. Kingſbury
Mrs. Kynaſton

L

Wm. Ludlow; Eſq.
Major Le Marchant
Mr. T. Lys
Mrs. Le Hunt

M

Rev. Mr. Mant
Mr. Monſton
      C. Mills
      J. Mobbs
Mrs. Mills
      Meſſer
      Martin, ſen.
Miſs Morris

N

Mr. Noble, Mayor
Miſs Norris

P

Mrs. Pitt
Perkins
Mifs Purbeck

R

Mr. Rice
Mrs. Reed
Raymond

S

Rev. Mr. Scott
Capt. Samfon
Mr. Stappers
Sadleir
Mrs. Shorley
Simpkins
Mifs St. John

T

Mr. W. Taylor
Mrs. Thomas, 2 Copies
Tarrant
Taylor
Mifs Taylor
C. Taylor

V

Mrs. Valabra

W

Rev. Mr. Woodford
E. B. Wollftoncraft, Efq.
Mr. J. Ward
Waring, Surgeon
Wylds
Mrs. Watfon
Woodyear
Mifs Watts
Wallis

N E W P O R T.

A

R EV. Mr. Atkins
Mr. W. Angle

Mifs E. Abbott

B

Philip Ballard, Efq,
Mr. R. Brown
Bayly
Wm. Baker
R. Barlow
Wm. Bouzell
R. Baffett, Surgeon
Wm. Bouyell
Mrs. Ballard
E. Browfe
Mifs E. Bowden

C

Mr. Wm. Clarke
Richard Cooke
Tho. Cooke
Rt. Clarke, Attorney
R. Clarke, ditto
Cowlam, Surgeon
Wm. Cooke
Mrs. Crooke
Mifs Clarke
Clab

D

Rev. Wm. Dickenfon
Mr. Rich. Drake
Wm. Drake
P. Dodd
Day
Mrs. E. Duglas
S. Davidfon
Duckett
Daw

E

Mrs. Elliott

G

Capt. Grace
Mr. Gréves
J. Gumm
Mrs. M. Goodive
Gregory

H
Lady Holmes
Mr. Hull
Mrs. E. Hayward
Mary Hall
Haddon
Harman
Mifs Heaton

J
Mr. Jerom
J. Jolliffe
Wm. Jones
Mrs. Jolliffe

K
Mr. J. Kirkpatrick

L
Mrs. Lalow

M
Mr. Robert Miller.
J. Mallett
Mrs. Major

N
Mr. P. Nichols
Richard Newbery
Mrs. Noles

P
Capt. Pyott
Mr. Thomas Pittis
E. Partridge
W. Pedder
Porter
J. Perry
Mrs. Pinhorn
Popham
Frances Pike

R
Mrs. E. Roberts
J. Roberts
Rogers
Roch

S
Mr. Wm. Sheath

Mr. J. Smith
Mrs. Sheath
E. Simms
Mifs M. Shipman

T
Mr. Trattle, Mayor
J. Tiller
Wm. Tucker
Mrs. E. Trattle
Mifs M. Bridges

U
Mr. J. Upward

W
Rev. Mr. Worfley
Mr. John Welman
J. Wray
Mrs. M. Wavell
Wavell
Whitehead

C O W E S.

A
MR. Andrews
Mr. Afh
Mrs. Alley

B
Mr. Blackford
Mrs. Blandford
Mifs Banifter
Buttefworth
Bafkerville

C
Mr. Cufhen
J. Cooke
Civil
Chiverton
Wm. Cuthen
Mifs Corke

D
Mr. James Deacon
Deacon

Mrs.

Mrs. De la Francis
Miſs Daniells

F

Mr. Fabian
Mrs. Francis
Miſs Fabian

G

Mrs. Gely

H

Mr. Daniel Hill
    Wm. Holloway
    Harris
Mrs. Harrington
    Haddon
    Hewitt

J

Mr. Jackſon
    H. Jeves
Mrs. Jacob

K

Mrs. Kent

M

Mr. Malſett
Mrs. Mackenzie
    M'Culloch
    Maund

P

Mrs. Parkman

R

Mr. Roe
    Roſſey
    C. Rotſey

S

Mr. Shepherd
    Spreets
    Speden
Mrs. Sime
    Simms
    Stephens

T

Mr. Thomſon

W

Mr. J. Wellſtead
    Leonard Wincey
Mrs. Wincey

PORTSMOUTH.

A

Mr. Aylward
    Mr. Adams
Mr. Avery
    Adams
Mrs. Alford
    Alford
    Allcock
    Aſmond
    Allian
    Allian
    Adams
    Anſell
    Arnold

B

Mr. Burnett
    Barker
    E. Binſtead
    Brackſtone
    Baker
    Binſteed
    Baldy
    Boyes
Mrs. Broughton
    Boſee
    Brown
    Backhouſe
    Burrell
    Brain
    Bowley
    Ballard
    Beſt
    Burlace

Mrs.

Mrs. Brine
Bruges
Bolton
Buſkell
Barefoot
Bagnoll
S. Brown
Barton
Buſbridge
Burnett
Bacon
Biſſett
Byerley
Brain
Broughton
Miſs Bedford
Batchelor
Budden
H. Boiſrond

C

Sir John Carter
Rev. Mr. Cooley
Capt. Chalmers
Mr. Cowcher, Druggiſt
Wm. Cox
Compton
Cox
Carter
Wm. Carter
Cooley
Cooke
Carter
Curtis
Cuzens
Collins
Couſens
Charmon
Cox
Mr. Cockton
Coker
Mrs. Curier

Mrs. Chudleigh
Cunningham
Churcher
Charters
Cave
Criſp
Cowdery
Champion
Crow
Cooper
Coſins
Miſs Crookſhanks
Cocks
R. Cocks
Cobden
Cuallett

D

Mr. Deacon
Dewey
Danford
Davis
Mrs. Dawle
Dundaſs
Denton
Miſs Dawſon

E

Mr. Elliott
Edwards
Elgar
Miſs Elliott
Eyer

F

Mr. Freeman
Freeland
Floyd
Foond
Fincham
Ford
Fuller
Mrs. Frankling

Miss Fenn
    Fry

G

Mr. John Godwin, Mayor
    Greenway
    Gransmore, 2 Copies
    H. Grant
    Gauntlet
Mrs. Gray
    Grigg
    Gibbens
    Garrett
    Grossmith
    Gill
    Gregory
    Green
    Gillam
    Glandening
    Grafham
Miss Grant

H

Lady Hood
Lady Hamilton
George Huish, Esq.
Lieut. Holmes
Mr. Horsey
    Hay
    Hancock
    Holt
    Higgens, jun.
    Hickley
    Hobbs
    Hoar
    Haylor
    Hayne
    Hill
    Halsted
Mrs. Hector
    Hillyar
    Hurry
    Hulke

Mrs. Harward
    Hunt
    Hewett
    Hunter
    Hammond
    Hill
    Hawker
    Hendry
    Heslop
    Holdstock
    Hillyer
    Hollis
    Hammond
    Hart
Miss A. Hunt
    Hinton
    Herring
    Hornby

J

Mr. Johnson, Surgeon
    Jubber
    Jeffery

K

Mr. Kennett
    J. Kingett
Mrs. King
    Kember

L

Mr. Thomas Lyed
    Lawson
    Lear
    Legg
Mrs. Lyons
    Lawrence
    Ladd
    Loup
    Legg
    Leeke
    Long
    Lovell
    Luke

M

Rev. Mr. Morce
Mr. Muirhead
Meredith
Miall
Millard, Surgeon
Mitchell, ditto
Marſhalls
Morey
Martin
Morley
Morgan
Moran
Money
Mills
Mitchell
Meſſer
Monday
Mrs. Moriaty
Mountain
Mouatt
Merritt
Morſe
Macbean
Mayby
Moſes

N

Hon. Mrs. Napier, 3 Copies
George Nunns, Eſq.

O

Rev. Mr. Orange
Mrs. Oſborn

P

Admiral Sir Thomas Pye, 3 Copies
Mr. Player
Pike
Peers, Attorney at Law
Polhill
Primate
James Paſſard

Mr. Priſtock
Palmer
Perrin
Mrs. Palby, 2 Copies
Pearce
Purkis
Peace
Porter
Pitt
Pope
Pepper
Paſley
Poole
Porter
Miſs Poore

R

Mr. Reed
Ramſey
Rule
Rule
Mrs. Rowe
Read
Rookſby
Reading
Robſon
Read
Roe
Robertſon
Miſs Ramſay

S

Mr. Sabene
Scurth
Smith
Spencer
Smith
Sanders
Stephen
Stone
Spurrell
Mrs. Smith
Sharp

Mrs.

Mrs. Snook
Sibley
Smith
Skeat
Shugar
Smith
Stanton
Shepherd
A. Smith
Sandys
Simpson
Steill
Stephen
Miss Shaw
Shepherd

T

Mr. E. Turner
Tolfree
Taylor
Tribe
Tattum
Teed
Trend
Mrs. Temple
Taylor
Thomson
Temple
Tracy
Miss Treleven
Teesdale

U

Mr. Upton
Vidol
Veck
Mrs. Vass
Miss Varlo

W

Mr. Weston
Wheeler
White
G. White

Mr. Woolfe
White
Williams
Willson
Watkins
Wade
White
Wallis
Mrs. Wisdom
Williams
White
Wiggins
Webb
Woodman
Whitly
Winson
Whitiar
Whitfield
Whetaker

Y

Mrs. Yatman

GOSPORT

A

MR. Adams
Mrs. Arminer
Mrs. Ashford
Allan
Adgman

B

Mr. Biddlecomb
Blamire, 2 Copies
Badge
Boys
Billett
Burnett
Beaty
Bonar
Mrs. Bird
Barton
Bradly

Mrs.

Mrs. Badge
    Boulton
    Ball
    Buckland
    Bowden
Miss Bedford
    Bligh
    Buckland
    Bingham
    Blundells

C

Vincent Corbet, Esq.
Mr. Collins
Mrs. Castleman
    Collins
    Crease
Miss Curry
    Carter

D

Lady Douglas
Mr. Danford
    Dods
    Drane
Mrs. Dalton
    Duncan
    Daman

E

Admiral Evans, 3 Copies
James Evans
Mrs. Ellison
    Elliott
Miss Eldridge

F

Mr. Robert Faulkner
Mrs. Figg
    Finsby

G

Mr. Grist
    Gilbert
    Grey
Mrs. Graham

Mrs. Goodriff
    Grist

H

Mr. Huish
    Harper
Mrs. Hill
    Hayter
    Handely
    Hendley
    Hall
    Hanly
Miss Howford
    Hollis

J

Mr. Jellicoe
    Jewell
Mrs. Jordan
    Johnston
    Jurd

K

Mr. Kneller

L

Mr, Ledgard
    Ledstone
Mrs. Lewis
Miss Lowley
    Lee

M

Mald. March
Mr. Midford
    Morse
    Marchall
    Mason
Mrs. Marshall
    Mason
    Moubrey
    Merritt
    Matthews
    Mason
Miss Mountford
    M'Kindey

N

N

Mr. Neilfon
Norrifh
Mrs. Norris

O

Mr. Orchard

P

Mr. Wm. Page
Parker
Mrs. Pedder
Parfons
Mifs Peachy
Piercy

R

Mr. Redman
Mrs. Roberts
Rook
Reeves
Mifs Roper
Randall

S

Mr. Smith
Smith, jun.
Mrs. Stanfield
Salt
Sutton
Shoveer
Salter
Silvefter
Simpfon
Mifs Searley
Shivers

T

Mr. Timmings
Mrs. Tither

U

Dr. Vaughan
Mrs. Vaughan
Veafey
Vaines
Underwood

Mrs. Utterfen

W

Mr. Wilkinfon
J. Wigley
John Whitear
Whitcomb
Weftbrook
Weft
Waller
Mrs. Waddy
Woodman
Waldron, 2 Copies
Wareham

Y

Mrs. Young

FAREHAM.

A

MR. Albeck
Mrs. Altarrow

B

Lady Benett
Mr. Barney
Blutherwick
Mrs. Bargus

D

Lady Dent
Mrs. Duglas

F

Mr. Franklin
Mrs. Franklien
R. Fall

G

Mr. Goodive
Mrs. Gayton
Godein

H

Mr. Henderfon
Mrs. Hodge
Hobfon

Mifs

Miss C. Hawker

J

Mrs. Johnson

K

Mr. Knight
John Knight
Miss Kneller

M

Rev. Mr. Mercer
Mr. Mason
Mrs. Montagu

N

Mr. Newman

P

Mr. Parsons
Perry
Mrs. Parsons
Porter
Phillips
Miss Parker

R

Mr. Ralfs

S

Mr. Sparkes
Mrs. Stares

T

Mr. Thresher
Miss Taylor

W

Rev. Mr. Wools
Mr. Wiglesworth
Mrs. Wallis

WICKHAM.

MR. English
Mr. Prior
Capt. Weir
Mrs. Atkins
Bradburn
Callaway

Mrs. Garnier
Maidman
Tyrwhitt
Woodrow
Miss Jacobs

WALTHAM.

REV. Mr. Bale
Mr. Bullock
Mr. Churcher
Cook
Cole
Donniger
Rev. Mr. Dusautoy
Mr. Fox
Jennings
Jonas
Capt. Lee
Mr. J. Penford
Richards
Villians
Rev. Mr. Walters
Mrs. Barfoot
Hart
Ann Jones
Woodman

ALRESFORD.

MR. Aslett
Mr. Bonall
Mr. Bradly
Bugby
Harley
John Hinden, jun.
Knapp
Rev. Mr. Masters
Lady Parker
Prangnall
Shawford
Soper

Mr.

Mr. Wright
    Wynn
Mrs. Aflett
    Buller
    Dancafter
    Edwards
    Green
    Harnefs
Mifs Fifher
    Holden
    Maria Holden
    Nevill
    Terry

NEWBURY.

SIR Jofeph Andrews
    Rev. Mr. Beft
——— Cooft, Efq.
T. Cowflad, Efq.
Mr. Hawkins
Capt. Howdell
Rev. Mr. Merchant
        Parry
Ofman Vincent, Efq.
Lady Andrews
Lady Craven, 3 Copies
Mrs. Davies
    Grigs
    King
    Merriman
    Penrofe
    Reidford
    Sainfbury
Mifs Hine
    May

ABINGDON.

MR. Bedwell
    Mr. Blake

Rev. Mr. Cleoburey
Mr. Curtis
    Jofeph Fletcher
    Thomas Fletcher
    Kent
Rev. Mr. Lake
Mr. Lewis
    Moore
Rev. Mr. Stevenfon
Mrs. Nafh
    Rofe
    Tomkins
    J. Tomkins
    W. Tomkins
    Tombs
Mifs Harding
    Kendall
    Stephens

WHITCHURCH.

MR. Barker
    Rev. Mr. Blair
Rev. Mr. Garnett
Jofeph Portal, Efq.
Mrs. Meadows
    Streatwell
    Thorngate
Mifs Hayter
    Philips

WOODSTOCK.

MR. Bennet
    Mr. Coles, Mayor
Rev. Mr. Hind
    King
    Kidding
Mrs. Brooks
    Ingram
    Scriven

Mrs.

Mrs. Walker, 2 Copies
Woodhull
Miss B. Ingram
M. Ingram

SALISBURY.

A

REV. Mr. Adams
Mr. Adams
Mr. Attwater
Hon. Mrs. Arundell
Miss Arundell
Attwater

B

Rev. Mr. Brown
Benson
Burch
Mr. Barfoot
Ballard
Biggs
Beale
Brownjohn
Mrs. Bearsley
Boucher
Best
Blake

C

Mr. Crosield
Curtoys
Coster
Carter
Causway
Mrs. Clarke
Cooper
Corfe
Crouch
Miss Chubb

D

Dr. Daniel
Mr. Dyke

Miss Dyker
Davis

E

W. B. Earle, Esq.
Mr. Edgar, jun.
Everett
Elliott
Mrs. Edwards
Miss Edwards

F

Mr. Fiddes
Freemantle
H. Freke
Forsyth
Mrs. Foster
Miss Fuller

G

Dr. Grove
Mr. Griesdale
Goulden
Green
Mrs. Goldwyre
Gibbs
Miss Grubbe
Goddard

H

Canon Hume
Rev. Mr. Holland
Colonel Hillman
Mr. Hawkins
R. Hawkins
Harris
Mrs. Hanham
Hussey
Hayter
Hodding
Hutfield
Miss Hawkins

J

Dr. Jacob
Mrs. Jeans

Mrs.

Mrs. Ivie
    Johnſon
Miſs Jacob
    Jukes
        L
Mr. Long
    Lewis
        M
Rev. Mr. Moore
Colonel Michel
Mr. Marſh
    J. Marſh
    D. Marſh
    Marks
    Merifield
    Mannings
Mrs. Martin
Miſs Moore
        N
Mr. Newton
Mrs. Noel
        O.
Mr. Ogden
        P
Francis Powell, Eſq.
Dr. Paul
Rev. Mr. Philips
Mrs. Pyle
Miſs Poore
    Prichards
        R
Mr. Rolfe
Mrs. Ridding
    Rolleſtone
    Rothwell
    Rooke
    Richards
Miſs Reed
    Rendall
        S
Nath. Still, Eſq. Mayor

Rev. Dr. Samber
Rev. Mr. Skinner
Mr. Shergold
    John Smith
    William Smith
    Sweatman
Mrs. Sympſon
    Sutton
    Slater
    Shuttleworth
    Sterne
Miſs Steele
        T
William Trenchard, Eſq.
Mr. Tanner
    Thatcher
        V
Mr. Vanderplank
        W
Rev. Mr. Williams
    Weſtcott
    Wyche
    White
    William Whitchurch
    Edmund White
    Wyatt
Mrs. Williams
    Wapſhare
    Wilkins
Miſs White
    Whitmarſh
    Weſtcott

ROMSEY.

CAPT. Wm. Brookman
    Mr. J. K. Comly
Mr. Thomas Hale
    J. Hedges
    Stephen Leach
    R. Newman
                Rev.

Rev. Mr. Penton
Mr. Richard Pearce
    W. Sharp
Rev. Mr. Williams
Mr. Watts
    Waldron
Mrs. J. Forder
    H. Godfrey
    S. Hardyman
    Pain
    Wells
Miss Cock
    Fletcher
    Madgwick
    Moller
    Tarver
    Trodd
    Whiting

B A T H.

A

DUCHESS of Ancaster
    J. Akers, Esq. 3 Cop.
Rev. Mr. Armstrong
Mr. Anstley
    Arundell
    Atwood
    Abbott
Mrs. Astley
    S. Albyn
B
Hon. Henry Bennet
Capt. Blacker
Mr. Barry
    Thomas Beale
    Bond
    Browne
    Bryant
    Burges
    O. Bush

Lady Baynton
Mrs. Baker
    Battin
    Baldwin
    Bennet
    Bennet
    Bennett
    Boldwon
    Beale
    Bowdler
    Burge
    Burr
    Barry
    Buckworth
    Bell
    Bunney
Miss Brock
    Blacker
C
Lord Conyngham
Rev. Mr. Collins
Capt. Cooke
Mr. Collings
    Colborne
    Cadby
    Crawford
    Cruttwell
    Cullais
Mrs. Cunlieffe
    Colborne
    Cotes
    Cocknone
    Campbell
    Collett
    Carne
    Cracroft
    Crowe
    Caink
    Chapman
    Cowper
Miss Coker

Miss

Miſs Clutterbuck
 Croſbie
 Creſſwell
D
Dr. Dobſon
Wm. Davifon, Eſq.
Mr. Dawſon
Mrs. Dawſon
 Dunne
 Dunne
 Deane
 Dory
 Dawſon
 Dimond
 Dart
Miſs Dobree
E
Lady Erne
Rev. Mr. Elderton
Mr. Elliot
Mrs. Evans
 Elton
 Edwards
Miſs Enys
F
Lady Fetherſton
Dr. Falconer
Thomas Falconer, Eſq.
Mr. Franks
Mrs. Forbes
 Forbes
Mrs. Fairfax
 Forman
Miſs Falkner
G
Rev. Mr. Griffith
 Gutteridge
Lady Glynn
Mrs. Glynn
Lady K. Gerald
Hon. Mrs. Grenville

Mrs. Gage
 George
 George
 Gyde
 Grimes
Miſs Greenwood
H
Counteſs of Howth
Lady Hervey
Hon. Mr. Hamilton
Col. Hunter
Rev. Mr. Hickes
Mr. Hagard
 Hetwell
 Harris
 Harmer
 Hepburn
Mrs. Holman
 Haggitt
 Hull
 Holcombe
 Harris
 Hoare
 Haward
 Hawkins
 Hetwell
 Haſſard
 Hancocke
 Humphreys
 Hedges
 Henſhaw
Mrs. Hinxman
Miſs Hayward
 Henton
 Hallifan
 Harriſon
 Haſſall
J
Mr. James
Mrs. James
 James

Mrs.

Mrs. Jackson
    Johnson
Miss Jackson
    Jones

K

Mr. Kilvert
    King
Mrs. Krauter
    Keasberry
Miss King

L

Lord Lisle
Lady Lisle
Mr. Lechmere
    Lowfield
Mrs. H. Lisle
    Linddiard
    Lawford
    Le Merchant
    Lee
    Le Mesurier
Miss Leigh
    Lewis

M

Lady Mannock
Hon. Mrs. Mackworth
Hon. Mrs. Moore
William Madden, Esq.
Thomas Mead, Esq.
Colonel Mackintosh
Rev. Mr. Morgan
Mr. M. Martin
    William Matthews
Mrs. Mackworth
    Munison
    Morgan
    C. Morgan
    Metholl
    Martin
    Morris
    Melmoth

Mrs. Martyn
    Moody
    Mayler
Miss Mendes
    S. Mendes
    Martin

N

Mrs. Negle
    Newman
    Needham
Miss Newcome

O

Mrs. Onslow
Miss Owen

P

Gen. Parslow
James Put
Mrs. Poole
    Petty
    Preston
    Peake
    Porter
    Procton
Miss Pearce
    Purlewent
    Plunkett

R

Mr. Russell
    Rack
Mrs. Ross
    Roebuck
    Robins
Miss Rumbouilet

S

Lady Sydney
    Stepney
    Mary Stanley
    Isabella Stanley
Sir John Stapylton, Bart.
Dr. J. Smith
Dr. Staker

Mr

Mr. J. Symons	Miſs Tyler
Stroud	Torre
Stracey	Taylor
Mrs. Snee	V
Savage	Mrs. Vandewall
Stone	Verker
Stewart	W
Saville	John Walcot, Eſq.
Simpſon	Rev. Dr. Wilſon
Smith	Dr. Watſon
Miſs Stanley	Mr. Wingrove
Swinburne	Williams
T	Wilſon
Right Hon. Lady Tracy, 2 Copies	Mrs. Warwick
	Wheeller
Capt. Tompſon	Welch
Mr. Thomſon	Wignall
Tully	White
Townſend	Wild
Timbrel, 2 Copies	Miſs Waters
Mrs. Thomſon	Wrey
Threſher, 2 Copies	Wiltſhire
Torrent	White
Trigg	Watts
Toundrow	Wingrove

⁎ It is hoped no Offence will be taken by any of the Subſcribers, ſhould any of their Names be improperly ſpelt, or their Titles of Diſtinction omitted, as the Author had not the Honour of knowing many of them.

(iv)

POEMS

Ano-

On

THE CONTENTS.

A   On

POEMS

ON VARIOUS OCCASIONS.

The AUTHOR's PLEA.

WHO with a Critic's eye this book
      runs o'er,
Detects perhaps, a thousand faults, and more,
Impartially the Author's plea must hear,
And then perhaps will ceafe to be fevere.

When reafon firft adorn'd my infant mind,
To books and poetry my heart inclin'd,

B   And

And as my years advanc'd, the paffion
    grew,
And fair ideas round my fancy flew.
The Mufes feem'd to court me for their
    friend,
But Fortune would not to their fuit attend;
She underftood who proper fubjects were,
To hold a converfe with thefe airy fair,
Muft be poffefs'd at leaft of independence,
That to the Mufes they may give at-
    tendance,
By books and ftudy fructify the mind,
And lead the genius where it was inclin'd.
The inaufpicious Dame deny'd that I,
Should thus, where Nature's felf inclin'd,
    apply;
For fhe perceiv'd, I did the Mufe befriend,
And could my days in contemplation fpend,

                         Yet

Yet fo contracted, circumfcrib'd my line,
I paus'd—if to difcard the tuneful Nine.

Now duty calls my thoughts a different
     way ;
Juftice enjoins ; I muft her call obey.
So when the Mufes come on anxious wing,
Some pleafing fubject to my fancy bring,
I bid them fly where peaceful leifure refts,
I have no time to entertain fuch guefts.
They oft affect a deafnefs, draw more near,
Declare that they can no repulfes bear,
Demand admittance, vow they are inclin'd,
To ftay till they imprint it on my mind.

Sometimes they are lefs bold, more fhyly
     come,
And with indiff'rence afk if I'm at home.

If

If duty will admit, I afk them in,
When fome engaging converfe they begin;
But ere, perhaps, the converfation's o'er,
Duty commands that we converfe no more.
Now Duty's call, I never muft refufe,
I rife,—and with a blufh myfelf excufe;
Tell them I muft withdraw a while, and
   when
Duty admits, I will return again.
Sometimes till I return, they deign to ftay,
Sometimes they take offence, and fly
   away,
And never on that fubject vifit more,
But bid me Fate's contracted hand deplore.

Thus, what the Author to the World
   prefents,
Appears through numberlefs impediments;
         And

And what of praife, or of difpraife you view,
To Nature and the Mufe is wholly due;
This, fhe prefumes, will candid minds
     fuffice,
And for her each defect apologize.

On LOVE and WINE.

Written by Defire of P. G. Efq. of

WINCHESTER.

COME, defcend ye gentle Nine!
  Be Cupid too and Venus there;
When I fing of Love and Wine,
  Let Bacchus to my fong repair.

Love, of ev'ry theme the beft;
  Where this celeftial paffion reigns,
Oh! the houfe, the heart, how bleft,
  Silken bands are Hymen's chains!

Love will ev'ry fault conceal,
  And kindly each defect pafs o'er;
Generoufly each good reveal,
  And the minuteft grace explore.

        Thofe

Thofe who wed for nought but gold,
    As well may marble rocks unite;
In their flinty cliffs enfold,
    And know Love's rapt'rous foft delight.

But when hands in wedlock join,
    And their twin'd hearts unite in Love;
Peace is their's, and joys divine,
    Next to thofe which reign above.

And fhould more aufpicious fate
    Beftow another bleffing ftill;
Deign our comforts to compleat,
    Our boards with Wine and Plenty fill.

Wine will chear the languid heart,
    And Love each angry thought controul
All that Nature afks, impart,
    And fill with Paradife the Soul.
                    Written

Written by the Defire of the Mifs B——s,
of WINCHESTER, on their parting with
Mr. and Mrs. G———N.

A H! gloomy, inaufpicious day,
      Which tears our charming friends
   away,
Which bids us from our G——N part,
And ftamps their abfence on our heart!
Let clouds and darknefs veil the fky,
And tears defcend from ev'ry eye.

   Adieu ye lovely happy pair,
Who all the focial comforts fhare;
Love, joy, and calm tranquillity,
Compofe your bleft fociety.

                              With

With you what happy hours we've ſpent,
In pleaſure, mirth, and ſweet content.
Alas ! thoſe pleaſing days are o'er,
And you the B————s bleſs no more.

But abſence ſhall not damp our flame,
Friendſhip's pure lamp ſhall burn the ſame;
And while we have an ear to hear,
The name of G————n ſhall be dear.

To

To a Young Gentleman who prefented
the Author with a Poem, in Commen-
dation of her Singing.

COULD I, arch youth, your flatt'ring
        lines believe;
Were not your fex too fubject to deceive,
I, like a credulous, unthinking maid,
Might be to thoughts of vanity betray'd ;
But, confcious my dull pipe no merit
    claims,
My foul, like a ftern oak, unmov'd re-
    mains.

Were I affur'd that what thofe lines im-
    part,
Was quite the genuine language of your
    heart,

                    It

It furely would *demonftrate* a defect,

Which in my friend I wifh not to detect.

Your fenfe and judgment 'twould at once
decry,

And prove you praife you know not what,
nor why.

But I efteem your fenfe and penetration,

And thus conclude, from that confideration,

That all th' encomiums you on me beftow,

I, to your fkill in irony muft owe ;

Your fex are quite proficients in this fchool,

And may elate the vain, unwary fool.

While I good-nature in my friend admire;
While grace and perfpicuity confpire,
To make him all a parent can defire,
Yet would I fay, as to the friend I love,
(For none fo good but he may ftill improve)
Would

Would you be thought a pleafing, hopeful
　　youth,
Let all you write or fpeak be grac'd with
　　truth.
Truth with refplendent luftre fhews her
　　face,
While falfhood fkulks, and finks in black
　　difgrace.
As you advance in years, in virtue grow,
So fhall you her tranfcendant bleffings know·
Virtue and Wifdom are entwined friends;
Who Virtue gains, true Wifdom appre-
　　hends,
Heav'n guards his feet, and peace his
　　fteps attends.

Spoken

Spoken extempore to a young Lady, whose
   Name was ORGAN, on her Return Home,
   after a few Months Abſence.

WHEN tuneful inſtruments appear,
    They indicate ſome pleaſure near,
And if an Organ we behold,
It doth a ſacred theme unfold ;
It's one, it's chief, it's grand deſign,
Is to break forth in ſongs divine.
Welcome, fair inſtrument of praiſe,
Thy preſence ſhall our ſpirits raiſe ;
And that thou art preſerv'd from ill,
Art an unblemiſh'd Organ ſtill,
That ev'ry pipe's in tune, rejoice,
And we'll accord in heart and voice.

C   THE

THE

WOMAN's ORNAMENT.

SYLVIA, as you descend from line to
      line,
I know your judgment will concur with
      mine.
Should passion with your better thoughts
      contend,
In Reason's empire I've insur'd a friend.
While I attempt, tho' in a feeble strain,
My sexes brightest ornament t' explain.

It centers not in yon' unthinking lass,
Who murders half her moments at the
      glass.
                      That

That well dreft cap, or better frizzled
    head,
With richeft pearls and tow'ring plumes
    o'er-fpread,
That lovely eafy fhape, or graceful air,
Which at the ball eclipfes all the fair,
That Angel's face, whofe beauteous hues
    difclofe,
The fnowy lilly, or the blufhing rofe;
With iv'ry teeth, or more bewitching
    eyes,
Before whofe luftre ev'ry brilliant dies;
With voice harmonious, or enchanting
    tongue,
With pointed wit, or elocution hung;
With thefe, O Sylvia! you may be replete,
Yet want the pearl which makes you truly
    great.

But can you boaft of wealth and ftore of
 gold?

In you, fome fordid minds the gem behold;

Poffeft of this, you'll meet each fwain's
 refpect,

It ftrangely turns to beauty each defect,

Makes prudence, virtue, fenfe, and merit
 flow,

From ground where folly, vice, and malice
 grow.

But one efteem'd the wifeft of the wife,

Beheld our fexes worth with other eyes,

And her pronounces, of the pearl poffeft,

Who's with a meek and quiet fpirit bleft,

Whofe foul retains found judgment, folid
 fenfe,

And virtue, with religion's noble fence;

An humble, generous, free, exalted mind,

From all the groffer fentiments refin'd;

        An

An heart fincere, fedate,—not apt to roam,
A mind domeftic, ever beft at home,
Be this my lot, my noble portion this,
And lo! I afk for no fuperior blifs.

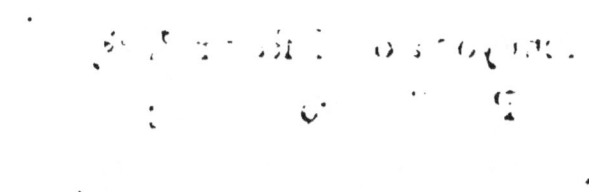

CREDULIA's

CREDULIA's COMPLAINT.

AH! why thefe tears,—this rifing figh,
  Thefe foft impreffions yet;
Cannot fuch matchlefs perfidy
  Compel me to forget?

Ye rural walks, ye verdant meads,
  Ye folitary bowers,
Beneath your foft alluring fhades
  I've kill'd unnumber'd hours.

From you alone I feek redrefs,
  Perfidious vows recal;
Perhaps you'll pity my diftrefs,
  For you have heard them all.

             Ah!

Ah ! with what tears did he invoke,
    What fighs my love implore,
A thoufand tender things he fpoke,
    And look'd a thoufand more.

Long did he feek CREDULIA's heart,
    Ere fhe that heart could give,
Till Cupid fhot that fatal dart,
    Which bade PERFIDIO live.

Now words were wanting to exprefs
    The tranfports of his foul,
He hop'd no more,—muft die with lefs,
    Her will fhould his controul.

Still more as with her converfe bleft,
    The gentle flame increas'd ;
'Twas Paradife within his breaft,
    When her his arms embrac'd.

                    And

And fhould fhe ever prove unkind,
    Or with another wed,
He'd never change his ftedfaft mind,
    But join the peaceful dead.

I heard nor did the fraud detect,
    The treach'rous fwain believ'd,
Nor once did my weak heart fufpect,
    I e'er fhould be deceiv'd.

But fuch I was ;—Yet ftill the tear
    Unwilling fills my eye,
And ftill I find his image here,
    And ftill I heave a figh.

But rife, my foul, with juft difdain,
    Regard the guilty youth,
Nor let him give thy bofom pain,
    Who flies the path of truth.

On

On the Marriage of a LADY, to whom the
Author was Bride-Maid.

A S the light bark on the tempeſtuous ſea,
Toſs'd to and fro, from dangers never
free;
Diſmay'd with fear, and mov'd with ev'ry
blaſt,
Till in a port her anchor's firmly caſt;
So oft is mov'd Man's fluctuating mind,
Till it in wedlock a ſafe anchor find;
Here, if the ſoul meets but her deſtin'd
mate,
Her joys are full, her happineſs compleat.

Be this your happy lot, my lovely friend,
Whoſe nuptial rites I this glad morn
attend;

Whoſe

Whose humble, gentle mind for peace was
     born,

Whom virtue, love, and innocence adorn.

Celestial graces dignify thy soul,

While pure religion all thy ways controul.

These noble virtues, which in thee abound,

Are haply in thy lov'd PHILANDER
     found.

His heart sincere, his temper soft and
     mild,

Nor torn by anger, nor with art beguil'd.

Such gentle hearts alone should join their
     hands,

And find that Hymen's chains are silken
     bands.

Their emulation's not who'll reign su-
     preme,

But who shall love the most,—be most
     serene.

                  Remote

Remote from vanity and wordly toys,
Each feeks with each for more fubftantial
     joys.
Tranquillity fhall in their borders dwell,
Nor difcord once approach their peaceful
     cell;
But mutually each other's grief they'll bear,
As mutually each other's joys will fhare.

Thus, thus, my friend, may you for
     ever prove,
The foft delight of harmony and love;
May ev'ry blelling you can afk of Heav'n,
To conftitute your happinefs be giv'n.
If Heav'n beftows, with joy receive the
     prize,
If Heav'n witholds, 'tis beft what Heav'n
     denies.

                               Thus

Thus sweetly may you pass your future
       life,

Nor once repent that you became a wife;

That you declin'd the pleasing name of

    B——m,

And that alone preferr'd of H——rag—m.

From

From EUSEBIA to FIDELIO.

ERE you, FIDELIO, thefe foft lines
        fhall view,
We fhall have fpoke that painful word,
        Adieu!
I know the anguifh of your faithful heart,
I know you thought it more than death to
        part;
But now 'tis done ;—The dreaded trial's
        o'er,
Your lov'd EUSEBIA you behold no more.
No more on willing feet together walk,
  'r of our joys, or of our forrows talk;
'' 'hen each, as to a friend fincere and kind,
D.. los'd the fond emotions of the mind.

D

No

No more FIDELIO's arms become my bed,
Or on his neck reclines my drooping head ;
Days, weeks, and months muft in fucceffion
      glide,'
Ere you, again, will join EUSEBIA's fide.
O'er hills and dales fhe takes her diftant
   · flight,
And mountain tops obfcure her from your
      fight;
Long lanes, and fields, and meadows
      cloath'd in green,
And many a weary ftep, lies now between.

Perhaps, ere this, a tear bedews your eye,
And your fad bofom heaves a tender figh;
But fpare your tears, of this your heart
      affure,
Mine eyes enough for you and I procure.

So

So let no doubts your conſtant heart aſſail,
For none but you, FIDELIO, ſhall prevail.
Shou'd Heav'n advance me to the higheſt
  ſphere,
You only are, and ever ſhall be dear.
That gen'rous heart, which ſought not
  gold, but me,
Shall meet its equal, noble, gen'rous, free.
Fair Fortune ſmiles and I'll again return,
And bid my juſt FIDELIO ceaſe to mourn.
Our conſtant hearts, our willing hands ſhall
  join,
Thy lov'd EUSEBIA ſhall be wholly thine.
But if on earth we ne'er ſhall meet again,
In this afflictive world of grief and pain;
If Heav'n, all-wiſe, erects my nuptial
  bed,
Within the peaceful regions of the dead,

I hope to meet you in that world above,

Where it will be adjudg'd no crime to
love;

Where *fathers* cannot frown, nor friends
difmay,

But all be joy through one eternal day.

On

On the Marriage of Captain A——— to
Mifs R———.

YE Nymphs of Helicon, attend my
lyre,
While all the feather'd Chorifters confpire,
In notes celeftial to falute the morn,
When SYLVIA doth the nuptial rites adorn.
See Cupids, Sylphs, and Goddeffes defcend;
Venus and all her gentle train attend;
While ev'ry fragrant flow'r appears in
bloom,
And minds moft penfive diffipate their
gloom.
All happy in this nuptial joy to fhare,
And each congratulates the happy pair.

D 3 The

The happy pair, who, lock'd in Hymen's
    bands,
United hearts, ere they united hands.

   ORENZO's heart, to martial fields enur'd,
Who all the hostile acts of war endur'd,
One tender look from SYLVIA quite dif-
    arms;
But where's the bosom can withstand such
    charms?
When beauty, grace, and innocence com-
    bin'd,
T' inspire the soul, and captivate the mind.
Who proof remains, 'gainst cannon balls
    and fire,
May by one glance from SYLVIA's eyes
    expire.
Those lovely eyes emitted such a dart,
As made a conquest of ORENZO's heart;

A noble conqueſt, worthy of the fair,
Who in his future joys and grief will ſhare.

  How bleſt the ſwain, of ſuch a bride
    poſſeſt !
The nymph ally'd to ſuch a ſwain, how
    bleſt !
Long may you live,—connubial life adorn ;
Yea, live to bleſs the children yet unborn,
Live,—and no other emulation know,
But who the greateſt tenderneſs ſhall ſhew ;
And when fair SYLVIA feels a Mother's care
May ſhe a Mother's conſolation ſhare ;
May ev'ry tender branch that ſhall be giv'n,
Be fructify'd with all the gifts of Heav'n.
While SYLVIA, who by good example's
    taught,
Whoſe mind is by maternal wiſdom
    fraught,
       With

With such instruction, as pursu'd through
    life,
Will grace the mother, and adorn the wife.
Fair SYLVIA will, with notions most refin'd,
Direct their steps, and cultivate the mind.
ORENZO too, with a paternal heart,
Will all that's useful, kind, or good,
    impart.
Thus, with each joy, and social comfort
    blest,
Each morn they'll rise, and eve retire to rest.

Should duty, loyalty, or war's alarms,
Demand ORENZO from his SYLVIA's arms,
With rage redoubl'd, he'll engage the foe,
And sink them swiftly down to shades
    below;
Bid each the fatal consequences prove,
Who dares detain the hero from his love.

Thus

Thus conqu'ring more by Cupid than by
      Mars,
Fly to his fair triumphant from the wars;
Find in her virtuous arms that sweet repaſt,
Which lawleſs libertines can never taſte;
Her ev'ry look ſhall joys ſublime create,
And make a Paradiſe of his retreat.

A

A

LETTER to an AUNT.

DEAR Madam pleafe to pardon me,
	That I with you this freedom take,
But thus a kind enquiry,
	After your health is all I make.

My parents, felf, and fifters too,
	Thro' mercy are extremely well;
And hope, and long, and pray that you,
	This pleafing news may have to tell.

Alas ! tis more than fix long years,
	Since you and I were forced to part,
I need not tell, for fure my tears
	Confefs'd how much it moved my heart.

This

This penfive thought my mind impreft,
    Alas! I ne'er fhall fee her more;
Then was my fpirit fo diftreft,
    That fill'd with grief, my eyes ran o'er.

And now again, with grief I fay,
    I ne'er expect your face to fee,
Since nothing calls me hence your way,
    And nothing calls you thence to me.

But if we never meet below,
    While we thefe mortal bodies wear,
When you, dear Aunt, to Heav'n fhall go,
    May I be bleft to meet you there.

While yet appears your fetting fun,
    Some fleeting moments yet remain;
If ev'ry family fhould be one,
    Why may not ink our paper ftain.

                      Madam,

Madam, if you will condefcend
    To write, if but a fingle line,
You'll much oblige your loving friend,
    An humble fav'rite of the Nine.

But fhould I not this favour gain,
    Till Death tranfmits me to my grave,
I wifh, dear Madam, to remain,
    Your loving dutious niece, JANE CAVE.

On

On the Departure of a Youth from the
Author, with whom fhe had lived near
two Years.

DAYS, weeks, and months are gone
    and paft,
This morning ufhers in the laft ,
The laft,—that ever we, my friend,
May in one habitation fpend.
But ere we part, my friendly mufe
Wou'd kindly this precaution ufe.

  You now are juft in manhood's dawn;
And flow'ry profpects deck the lawn ;
Wealth, pleafure, ftrength, and length of
    days,
With joyful hope, your mind furveys.

                    E   But

But let your heart receive this truth,
Ten thoufand fnares are laid for youth;
Ten thoufand fins, in pleafure's drefs,
Each youth will to their bofom prefs.
One fin calls here, another there, ⎫
And youth, too oft, incline an ear, ⎬
The foft delufive voice to hear. ⎭

    Regard then this my parting breath,
Thofe flow'ry paths lead down to death,
And when you are from me remote,
With gay companions, void of thought;
When you fhall hear their tongues profane
The great JEHOVAH's facred name,
And you, perhaps, with them fhall join
To imprecate the wrath divine,
Tho' no reproving friend is near,
Remember God himfelf is there.

                         Let

Let recollection then relate,
What oft you've heard a friend repeat,
Confcience fhall ev'ry truth atteft,
And own each admonition juft;
She will a faithful diary keep,
Tho' oft we think fhe's lull'd to fleep.
But ah !—fhould death your foul o'ertake,
You'd find the treach'rous dame awake;
But this obfcure, this laft fad day,
Youth fhuns, and puts it far away.
But come, or foon, or late that hour,
We know we all muft feel its pow'r.

This long expected period's come,
As certain *that,* which feals our doom,
Which ftabs our vitals,—draws our breath,
And clofes up our eyes in death,
Which makes us bid the world Adieu !
And brings eternity to view,

Which

Which hails us partners of the fky,
Or bids us down to horror fly :
Then fhall your heart thefe lines approve,
And know that all I meant was love.

Written to a Friend, on going to ITCHEN,
about five Miles from WINCHESTER, to
fee a Country Seat belonging to the Duke
Chandos.

A Friendly party, of one mind,
Were for a pleafure-day inclin'd,
Forfook their beds on Thurfday morn,
When each their perfons did adorn

With

With raiment proper for the day,
And in high fpirits drove away.

The morn did a bad day portend,
Bid fome unwelcome fhow'rs defcend;
But fable clouds now difappear,
And azure decks the atmofphere;
Phœbus expands his golden rays,
And all the rural fweets difplays,
And that my friend the whole may know,
We to a place call'd ITCHEN go;
Where, with an honeft batchelor,
We meet with good and hearty cheer.
Sincere, ingenuous, plain and free,
No needlefs compliment had he.
Each welcome, what he lik'd to chufe,
And each as welcome to refufe.
A while we after dinner fat,
Engag'd in inoffenfive chat,

E 3   Then

Then arm in arm, in pairs we ſtalk,
And to his Grace's manſion walk.
Here, each apartment we behold,
Doth ſomething of the Duke unfold.
Magnificence decks ev'ry place,
And ſpeaks the owner is his Grace.
Some ancient portraits caught my eye, ⎫
Which bid my boſom heave a ſigh,   ⎬
For ah! thoſe once lov'd forms with ⎭
     reptiles lie.

When we had view'd the manſion o'er,
Park, garden, fiſh-ponds, and much more,
Our feeble frames begin to tire,
And ſome refreſhment we require.
We now approach the humble cell,
Wherein our ruſtic friend doth dwell.
Here, fill'd with new ideas, we
Regale us with a diſh of tea.

Some

Some hours yet remain unfpent,
And pleafure was our fole intent.
So that we may the fame increafe,
Refolv'd the chryftal ftream to trace,
Forthwith into a boat we go,
And up and down the river row,
See the glad fifhes frifk and play,
And feem as bleft, and pleas'd as they.

 Re-ent'ring now our friends retreat,
To make his bounty quite compleat,
A pleafant fyllabub we find,
When each may drink, who is inclin'd.

 Phœbus now haftens to the weft,
We think to haften home is beft;
So parting with our gen'rous friend,
Wifhing each blifs may him attend,
Enter our carriage, drive away,
Beftow encomiums on the day.

       None

None feem'd inclining to relent,
Each had a day of pleafure fpent;
Thus chatting on, till we alight,
And bid each other a good night.

    Thankful, we all are fafe and well,
And that no ill has us befel;
Each to their dwelling go their way,
And thus concludes our pleafure-day.

A Poem, occafioned by a Lady's doubting
  whether the Author compofed an Elegy,
  to which her Name is affix'd.

IF good Mifs H— will condefcend,
   To read thefe lines which I have penn'd,
Perhaps it may her doubts confute,
And fhe'll no more my word difpute,
               But

But own I may the Author be,
Of what she did on Sunday see.

You'd hate a base perfidious youth,
Such *my* disgust to all untruth.
A gen'rous mind is never prone
To claim a merit not her own.
I wou'd disdain t' affix my name
To that, which is another's claim.
Of beauteous form Heav'n made me not,
(Nor has soft affluence been my lot,)
But fix'd me in an humble station,
Remote from those of rank and fashion;
But there are beauties of the mind,
Which are not to the great confin'd;
Wisdom does not erect her seat
Always in palaces of state;
This blessing Heav'n dispenses round,
She's sometimes in a cottage found,

And

And tho' she is a guest majestic,
May deign to dwell in a domestic.

  Yet, of this great celestial guest,
I dare not boast myself possest,
But this wou'd represent to you,
As Wisdom does, the Muses do,
No def'rence shew to wealth or ease,
But pay their visits as they please.
Sometimes they deign to call on me,
And tune my mind to poetry ;
But ah ! they're fled, I'll drop my pen,
Nor raise it till they call again.

A

A POEM for CHILDREN.

On Cruelty to the Irrational Creation.

OH! what a cruel wicked thing,
   For me who am a little King, *
To give my haplefs fubjects pain,
And make them groan beneath my reign.

Were I a chafer, and could fly,
Ah! fhould I not with anguifh cry,
Should naughty children take a pin,
And run me through to make me fpin?

Were I a bird, took from my neft,
Should I not think myfelf oppreft,
If tofs'd about in wanton play,
'Till maim'd and faint I die away?

* See PSALMS, viii. vi.

Now

Now, and when I'm a bigger boy,
Let cruelty my heart annoy,
Becaufe it is a dreadful evil,
That only fits me for the Devil.

If I muft ought of life deprive,
The quickeft way I will contrive,
To ftop the tremb'ling victim's breath,
And give it little pain in death.

I'll not torment a dog or cat,
A toad, a viper, or a rat;
They're form'd by an Almighty hand,
And fprung to life at his command.

A bull, a horfe, yea every creature,
Of the moft mild or favage nature,
Were kindly given for my ufe,
But never meant for my abufe.

Good

Good men, thy holy word attefts,
Are kind and tender to their beafts;
May I be merciful and kind,
That I with thee may mercy find.

Written by Defire of a Lady, on an angry,
petulant Kitchen-Maid.

GOOD Miftrefs Difhclout, what's the
matter?
Why here—the fpoon, and there—the
platter?
What demon caufes all this low'ring,
Black as the pot you oft are fcow'ring?
Hot as the fire you daily light,
Your fpeech with low invectives blight,

F

While

While rage impregnates ev'ry vein,
And dies the face *one crimfon ftain.*

   Sure fome one has a word mifplac'd,
Or look'd not equal to your tafte,
Or, is this juft the time you've chofe,
Your great acquirements to difclofe,
Difplay the graces of your tongue,
Shew with what eloquence 'tis hung,
As dog, rogue, fcoundrel, fcrub, what not,
And twenty more, I've quite forgot;
Which prove to a demonftration
You've had a lib'ral education;
Such titles muft enchant the ear,
And make the bounteous donor dear;
But while thefe bounties are difpenfing,
I wifh I'd learn'd the art of fencing,
Leaft while at John you aim to throw,
My nob fhould chance to catch the blow;

                    Then

Then I fhould get a broken pate,
And marks of violence I hate.

  Good Miftrefs Difhclout condefcend
To hear the counfel of a friend ;
When next you are difpos'd to brawl,
Pray let the fcull'ry hear it all,
And learn to know, your fitteft place
Is with the difhes and the greafe,
And when you are inclin'd to battle,
Engage the fkimmer, fpit, or kettle,
Or any other kitchen gueft,
Which you in wifdom might think beft.

    Written

Written by Defire of a Mother, who had
loft an only Child.

A S with delight we view the op'ning

Expand, and all her fragrant fweets difclofe,
So did MATERNA view her lovely maid,
In all the charms of innocence array'd;
Oft had her little all, her only child,
The tedious hour with pleafing chat
    beguil'd,
But Heav'n, all-good, and infinitely wife,
Remov'd this darling idol to the fkies,
Ere her young heart had been *obdur'd* by fin,
Or guilt, tormenting fiend, could brood
    therein,
Ere fhe arriv'd at years that might deftroy,
By one falfe ftep, a tender mother's joy.
                 Behold

Behold she soars to yon celestial fields,
Where ev'ry plant æthereal odour yields ;
With pitying eye, methinks she looks below,
Commis'rates a tender mother's woe,
Bids her dejected heart from earth retire,
And all her future thoughts to Heav'n
  aspire ;
Prepare, she cries,—prepare to meet the
  blest,
And join your SALLY in eternal rest.

On the Author's leaving BATH and going to
  WINCHESTER, Nov. 13, 1779.

ALAS! 'tis done, I can no longer stay,
  For Tuesday morn will hurry me
  away,

     From

From BATH,—from friends whofe friend-
    fhip I revere,
Friends—moft difint'refted and fincere;
I bid them all adieu! and go alone,
To a ftrange place, unknowing and un-
    known.
I know your kindeft wifhes me attend,
And in this place may raife to me a friend.

    I go,—but fome, alas! from whom I
        part,
Like a kind parent lie within my heart,
And cou'd I know we part, to meet no more,
I wou'd each thought of parting now give
    o'er.

    My tears prevent,—why do mine eyes
        o'er-flow,
And why my heart fuch poignant forrow
    know?

But

But can I,—dare I, unaffected be,
With such unmerited respect to me ?
I nought possess, I nothing can return,
But sure my heart with gratitude shall burn ;
Indelible *their* kindness shall remain,
Nor will I wish my passions to restrain.

My pray'rs and tears (would they were
    prevalent !)
Shall be to Heav'n by ardent breathing
    sent
That ev'ry wish'd for blessing may descend
On each whom kindness constitutes my
    friend ;
May plenty, life, and health with each
    remain,
And I be blest to meet you all again.

But should pale Death for either of you
    call,
Or fix on me, and force me from you all,

Be

Be this my pray'r, till my frail life is o'er,
That we may meet on yon celeftial fhore,
Where death, and grief, and parting are
    no more.

A Poem, on the Celebration of the Night
  in which Miffes W—— and J—— were
  bound Apprentices to Mifs H. BATH.

IN love and innocent delight
  We meet to fpend this wifh'd for night;
When FLAVIA and SELIME are bound,
And may their time with peace be crown'd.
May health and harmony, and love,
And all the bleffings from above,
Crown ev'ry day kind Heav'n fhall give,
Whilft you fhall with fair SILVIA live.

                     May

May FLAVIA, and young SELIME too
(As friends confiftently may do)
In this each other emulate,
Who fhall with knowledge be replete;
Who be moft active, moft fincere,
Who moft in goodnefs perfevere:
And whilft fair SILVIA rules with eafe,
Be your ambition ftill to pleafe.
So peace fhall crown your fleeting hours,
Content and happinefs be yours.

Written by the Defire of a Lady, On Building of Caftles.

BUILDING of Caftles did commence,
　　In days of old, for our defence,
And ufually erected were,
Adjacent to the Seat of war;

Where

Where blood and flaughter did abound,
And drench'd with gore the thirfty ground;
Where powder, darts, and bullets flew,
Nor one relenting paffion knew;
But winging through the fmoke and fire,
Made thoufands groan, bleed, and expire.

Caftles were built firm and fecure,
Wherein fome treafure to infure;
With cells and caverns dark, profound,
And walls impregnable around.
It's direful decorations are
The whole artillery of war;
Cannons and mufkets, fwords and bombs,
Hangers and fpears, and fifes and drums.
Bullets, and ev'ry fit fupply,
Wherewith t'attack the enemy.

Some caftles too, of which we hear,
Are fabricated in the air;

But

But thefe are of the mental kind,
The fole conftruction of the mind:
We in thefe æther caftles ride,
With all the equipage of pride,
And in imagination rife,
Superior monarchs of the fkies.
One blaft this edifice deftroys,
Abortive are our promis'd joys.

Our miniftry this caftle built,
By which the blood of thoufands fpilt;
Fancy'd a thoufand men or two
Could all AMERICA fubdue.
But thrice ten thoufand crofs'd the main,
A million's in the conteft flain.
Yet, ah! fell caftle, direful ill,
AMERICA's un-conqu'red ftill.

Caftles are an imperfect plan,
Of that fuperior creature,—Man,.

The

The body is a caftle where,
The moft'intrinfic treafures are ;
Well fraught with arms for man's defence
As reafon, recollection, fenfe ;
Which if we exercife aright,
Put all our Enemies to flight ;
Spoil Envy with her pois'nous dart,
And wound refentment to the heart ;
Bid Difcontent and Anger fly,
And each unruly paffion die ;
Subdue Diftruft and black Defpair,
And fubftitute Contentment there.
Thus conqu'ring, we fuperior rife
With fhouts of vict'ry to the fkies.
Where ev'ry Conqueror is bleft,
In Caftles of eternal reft.

The

The AUTHOR perfonates the MOTHER viewing the Portrait of Mr. T. W. who was then in the EAST INDIES.

L O! here the lovely portrait's feen,
    But, ah! what oceans roll between;
What tracks of land, and deferts-wild,
Divide me from my darling child!
Carnage, and Death triumphant reign,
Storms rife, and thunders roar in vain,
Nor rocks, nor racks, nor wars deter,
The dear, the bold Adventurer;
Difdaining affluence, peace, and eafe,
He braves the horrors of the feas.

    Thou, whofe omnifcient eye pervades
Celeftial heights, and darkeft fhades,
Surveys at once each point of land,
And holds the ocean in thy hand,

G   Preferve

Preferve this brave advent'rous youth,
And lead him to the paths of truth;
Still o'er his ev'ry thought prefide,
And bid his foul in thee confide.
Preferve him, till each danger's o'er,
And land him on his native fhore;
Then our exulting hearts fhall raife
A fong of gratitude and praife.

Written to an AUNT, accompanied with TWO ELEGIES.

MADAM, your Niece refumes her pen,
And writes to her dear Aunt again;
That you may fee her weak attempts,
Humbly two Elegies prefents.
Begs you will kindly them accept
With this precaution—don't expect

Any

Any great worth in them to fee,
For they were wholly made by me.
Tho' quite imperfect, don't refufe
The labours of a Female's Mufe,
But kindly each defect pafs o'er,
Your niece JANE CAVE will afk no more.

On feeing Lady P— at a Place of Worfhip.

MY flighted Mufe long time had flown,
    And great difguft to me had fhewn;
But yefterday fhe call'd again,
And forc'd me to refume my pen.
  " Behold! fhe faid, yon lovely face,
" Which Nature form'd with fo much grace,
" Riches and honours are her own,
" And focial comforts yet unknown,
" Prudence, that lov'd tho' humble gueft,
" Erects a throne within her breaft.

" When

" When plac'd within the Houfe of Pray'r,

" She recollected GOD was there;

" Tho' Levity was by her fide,

" She with a fweet becoming pride,

" Rebuk'd the fair——devoutly fat,

" Nor once prefum'd to laugh or chat:

" For well fhe knew 'twould fink her down

" Below the level of a Clown.

" That titles only agrandize,

" And bid us as fuperiors rife,

" In juft proportion as they're join'd,

" Unto a great ennobled mind;

" Who, with a proper, humble grace,

" Demeans herfelf in ev'ry place,

" Such is the fair of whom I fpeak,

" For whom I did this vifit make."

Thus fpake my Mufe, then took her flight

Inæther, and out foar'd my fight.

POEMS
SACRED TO THE
MEMORY of the DEAD.

On the Death of Mr. BRADFORD, an eminent Gardener in BRISTOL, July, 1774.

WHERE are thofe wonted feet, O tell
    me where!
That to this garden did fo oft repair?
Behold! I fearch, but ah! I fearch in vain,
Alas! no traces of them here remain.
    Ye plants and flow'rs, come tell me if
    you can,
Where is the good, laborious, faithful man,

G 3   Who

Who daily view'd you with difcerning
        eye,
Wou'd ev'ry beauty, ev'ry fault efpy?
Nect'rines and peaches, apricots and all
Ye pleafant fruits, that are within my call,
Where are thofe hands, that with an artful
        care
Oft prun'd your trees, knew when to prune,
        and where?
Hot-houfe and green-houfe, next I afk of
        you,
But ye unwilling are to tell me too.
Of ev'ry plant, and tree, and flow'r I afk,
But none will undertake the painful tafk,
The truly fatal, penfive news to tell,
To fay their friend has took his long
        farewel,
For all his lofs, in filent grief deplore,

                  Their

Their looks proclaim that BRADFORD is no
  more.

No more, methinks they say, we see our
  friend,

Who weeks, and months, and years with
  us did spend;

Who planted us, and set us first to grow,

Transplanted us, and mov'd us to and fro.

Us to improve, was BRADFORD's chief delight,

His work by day, and study too by
  night.

Before the rising of yon radient sun,

Each morn our friend his daily work begun.

Yea, oft with fair Aurora he would rise,

For us the soft alluring bed despise.

Now no such care and constancy we find,

Alas! his equal is not left behind.

       Whilst

Whilft thus the penfive flow'rs his worth
    repeat,
The plants and trees their cries reverberate:
And I'll their authenticity atteft,
His worth and merit were by all confeft,
He was labor'ous, careful, wife, and good,
Each plant and tree minutely underftood.
He was,—but ah! I'll not recount his praife,
'Twill not allay our grief, but forrow raife;
For now he is no more, but borne away,
From realms of forrow to celeftial day.
Propitious Heav'n beheld, and mov'd with
        love
Kindly remov'd him hence to realms above,
And when he found his diffolution nigh,
He faid, "Come, wife, fit down, and fee
        me die."
Serene and calm he bow'd his peaceful head,
Without a groan the willing fpirit fled.

                                And

And when this tranfitory life is o'er,
O may his partner gain the happy fhore,
Triumphant in a flaming car afcend,
And ever dwell with her departed friend!

On the Death of Mrs. MAYBERY, of BRECON.

AND can it be ? and is her fpirit fled ?
    Is dear OPHELIA number'd with the
    dead ?
Are all the days of her probation paft ?
And is her die unalterably caft ?
Heart piercing thought—flow tears from
    ev'ry eye,
While ev'ry bofom rifes with a figh.
What goodnefs, prudence, wifdom, laid in
    duft !
Ah! Who the greateft Potentate can truft!
                Where

Where's he! could I each mortal's name
    rehearse,
Who pow'r hath gain'd this sentence to
    reverse.

  Obdurate King—Insatiable Death!
Who thus a period puts to mortals breath;
By thy rude hand no defference is paid,
Greatness with indigence in dust is laid;
Destruction is essential to thy name,
And all thy direful acts thy pow'r pro-
    claim.
What hopes are spoil'd? What near con-
    nections broke,
By this thy sudden unrelenting stroke?
The life destroy'd, the valuable life
Of mistress, sister, daughter, mother, wife.

  See her domestics who her goodness knew,
Pour forth the tribute to her merit due,
                              While

While weeping fifters bath'd in tears remain,

And fighing brothers fcarce their grief
    fuftain.

While tender, aged Parents' hearts o'erflow,

Nor joy nor reft, nor confolation know,

While duteous children, fent her by the Lord,

In fruitlefs tears the mournful day record.

And then behold, but ah ! what heart can
    guefs

The grief profound, the depth of that diftrefs,

Which feiz'd at once the partner of her bed,

When told his wife, his other felf was dead ?

Trembling methinks, with ev'ry thought
    amaz'd,

Aftonifh'd at the meffenger he gaz'd !

The vital ftream congeals in ev'ry vein,

While fcarcely fpirits, ftrength, or life
    remain.

                         Anxious

Anxious at once the whole dread scene to
    know,
Yet dreads to hear what will increase his woe.
At length inform'd—delug'd in grief he lies,
Nor hopes redress, but from his weeping eyes.
He calls the friendly tear to ease his grief,
But these recoil, nor deign to give relief.
Thus with an heart o'erborne, and spirits
    broke,
He sinks beneath th'intolerable stroke.
He ruminates—at length the silence breaks,
And thus methinks, in pensive accents speaks;
Alas! for me, my happier days are o'er,
I hear the voice—behold the face no more
Of her my friend, my best belov'd, my wife,
The joy, support, and comfort of my life;
The tender mother of my progeny,
The prudent mistress of my family;

                   How

How many ufeful years might fhe have
    fpent,

To blefs thofe children, which by Heav'n
    are lent,

To guide their feet, inculcate filial fear,

While ev'ry look maternal love did bear ?

Her care judicioufly, rul'd all within,

When I, for weeks and months have abfent
    been.

My help-mate fhe, who with fuperior grace,

Adorn'd the miftrefs, wife, and mother's
    place.

Thus mourns her fpoufe, while numbers
    fwell the cry,

Her death demands a tear from ev'ry eye.

In her the poor and wretched found a friend,

On her did for their chief fupport depend.

Bleft with a noble, free, and gen'rous heart,

In her mean av'rice could claim no part.

        H   And

And now 'twould be but juſt, if in return
A flood of tears were pour'd upon her urn ;
While all thoſe grievances ſhe did redreſs,
Her name and memory for ever bleſs.

————————————————

On the Death of Mrs. BLAKE, of CROCK-
HORN, who died in a Week after being
ſafely delivered of the ſixth Child.

WHAT eye forbids a tear, what heart
a ſigh ?
Fly ſome auſpicious Angel, quickly fly !
The ſtroke is too ſevere for man to bear,
If ſome celeſtial comfort be not there.

How anxiouſly the lov'd EUSEBIUS ſtands,
To Heav'n in pray'r lifts up his ardent
hands;
That when the trying period ſhall arrive,
The dear AMATA be preſerv'd alive.

At

At length the hour advances, Heav'n feems
    kind,
And lo! a lovely infant foon we find;
The dear maternal friend bids fair for life,
And the fond hufband views his lovely wife,
The living mother of a living child,
And all the hufband all the father fmil'd;
Joy fills his heart, love fparkles in his eyes,
And each foreboding thought before him dies.
His grateful heart afcends in praife to Heav'n,
Whofe goodnefs had this double blefling giv'n.
Each friend congratulates the happy pair,
And wifhes in their mutual joy to fhare.
Life fmiles on all, no trouble feems t'annoy,
But ah! fad change—How tranfient is the
    joy?
Each heart where gladnefs fat—beneath the
    ftroke
Sinks to defpair, and all it's comfort's broke.

        Her

Her face, which yielded pleafure and delight,
At once turns pale and folemn as the night;
Gloom fpreads around, her Sun withdraws
    his rays,
And fets in the meridian of her days.
She meekly yields, finks from the fondeft
    arms,
She dies!—and with her die a thoufand
    charms,
  In her the moft endearing wife is dead,
The tend'reft mother from her children fled.
The courteous neighbour, faithful friend ⎫
    fhe prov'd,   ⎬
In life by all refpected and belov'd,   ⎭
By all lamented when from life remov'd.
Earth feem'd unworthy of her longer ftay,
And Heav'n receiv'd her to celeftial day;
There fhe beholds the glories of her Lord,
And all her virtues meet a full reward.

On

On the Much Lamented DEATH of the
Rev. Mr. WHITFIELD, who died in
NEW ENGLAND, Sept. 30, 1770.

WHY doth all Nature wear an awful
        gloom?
And why, alas! exults yon diftant tomb?
Why doth a fable cloud the fky o'er-fpread?
WHITFIELD alas! feraphic WHITFIELD's
        dead,
The Friend, the Chriftian, the approv'd
        Divine,
The Saint in whom the life of GOD did fhine,
The man whom Heav'n ordain'd to preach
        for all,
And thoufands by his miniftry to call;
The Lord did chufe him in his youthful
        days,
To fpeak his glory and fet forth his praife.

        H 3   Mov'd

Mov'd by celeftial love, did undertake,

The miniftry alone for Jesu's fake.

His tongue was touch'd with evangelic fire,

And heav'nly raptures did his foul infpire.

Then forth into the World this Herald came,

Refolv'd to propogate Immanuel's name ;

To fet his glory forth from pole to pole,

Were the capacious breathings of his foul.

He loudly did the Gofpel trumpet found,

Whilft thoufands trembl'd as they ftood
  around,

Proclaim'd the fuff'rings of a dying God,

Invited finners to his pard'ning blood,

Enforc'd to all the great neceffity

Of knowing this—" The Saviour dy'd for
  me."

Thus was our nation blefs'd with Gofpel
  truth,

Boldly deliver'd by this chofen Youth,

        Who

Who with an heart inflam'd with JESU's love,
Caus'd GOD to pour his bleffings from above.
But did this Champion for the living GOD,
Appear in England only, to do good?
No, no, his gracious Captain points his way
Beyond the feas, and Whitfield muft obey:
For in his Maker's will he did rejoice,
Was all attention to his facred voice.
When JESUS bade o'er raging feas to pafs,
Through vaft AMERICA, to found his grace,
There, like an Herald for the bleeding
   Lamb,
He went, and did the Negroes fouls inflame.
Shew'd Ethiopians their Redeemer nigh,
To cleanfe their fpotted fouls from deepeft
   dye.
In fuch pathetic accents mov'd his tongue,
As rent and broke the very heart of ftone.
       Thus

Thus did he found his Maker's praife abroad,

A lab'rer in the vineyard of his GOD.

But now, alas! his labours are all o'er,

The fields do eccho with his voice no more;

No more from his dear Englifh friends he
                parts,

No more returns to animate their hearts,

But leaves ten thoufand thoufands to deplore

The death of him, who lives to die no more.

Let things inanimate his worth proclaim!

And fhout from fea to fea his wond'rous
                name!

O ye nocturnal luminaries tell,

What love for fouls did in his bofom dwell!

Say, fay what nights this advocate with
                GOD

Spent wreftling to avert th'impending rod.

Let fair AURORA in her turn declare,

How he preceded her by praife and pray'r.

                                Let

Let churches, chapels, tabernacles tell,
Who e'er within their walls did him excel.
Let counties, cities, towns, and ftreets pro-
    claim,
How faithfully he did the truth maintain.
Say winds and waves, how oft the Saint ye
        tofs'd,
When he for God the great Atlantic crofs'd?
And let the Continent abroad begin,
To tell what heav'nly news he there did
        bring,
How he explain'd the love of Jesu's heart,
'Till finners with their ev'ry fin did part.
Hell trembl'd when this god-like man arofe,
And all its votaries commenc'd his foes.
Say, Prince Infernal, how inhanc'd thy ire,
When Jesus did his Whitfield's foul infpire;
When like a flaming Seraph round he flew,
Thy works, thy caufe, thy kingdom o'er-
    threw?
                                    Say,

Say ye celeftial Angels, how ye fled,

On willing wings, to guard his favour'd
      head.

Say, ev'ry Saint, how did your hearts rejoice,

When ere ye heard the found of W's voice;

Well might each bofom figh, each Chriftian
      weep,

When this feraphic herald fell afleep.

But could we quit thefe tenements of clay,

And foar aloft into celeftial day,

There faithful Whitfield may at once be
      found,

With an eternal wreath of glory crown'd,

And fhouting loud Hofannahs to that God,

Who made him more than conqu'ror thro'
      his blood.

May we, like him, each breath for Jesus
      fpend,

Like Whitfield perfevere unto the end,

                   Like

Like him fail through this life's tempeftuous
    fea,
Fight the good fight, and gain the victory:
That when the laft tremenduous trump fhall
    found,
We in the wedding garment may be found,
With Angels, Saints, and favour'd Whitfield
    meet,
And ever worfhip at IMMANUEL's feet,
There fing the wonders of redeeming love,
With all the blood-bought company above.

On the Death of the Rev. Mr. HOWELL

HARRIS, who died JULY 21, 1781.

WHAT penfive, folemn, dolefull tidings
    found?
All ZION's fons will deeply feel the wound!

A

A brother, friend, a father dear is gone!

HARRIS is dead; his crown of glory's won!

What tongue can tell, what hand can paint
  the lofs

Of one fo fteady under JESU's crofs?

Hail, happy foul! thy mourning days
  are o'er,

Inhabitant of mortal flesh no more!

No more shall pain and anguish thee confine,

Nor on a dying-bed thy head recline.

No more shall fin opprefs thy righteous foul,

Nor grief come near, while endlefs ages roll.

No more (when glows thy heart with pure
  defire)

Thou'lt feel the force of perfecution's fire.

No more, with what is worfe, shalt thou be
  try'd,

By vain Profeffors fetting thee afide:

Advanc'd

Advanc'd beyond their frowns, beyond their
  praife,

HARRIS with Angels tunes his grateful lays.

He fits with all thofe radiant hofts above,

And fwims in feas of pure celeftial love.

He meets his blefled partner, gone before,

They meet to praife their God, and part no
  more.

She like a brilliant diamond appears,

And helps to decorate the crown he wears.

Not her alone, but thoufands more there be,

Whom GOD awaken'd by his miniftry.

 How glorioufly he fhines ;—what mean
   thefe fighs?

Why flow thefe torrents from our languid
  eyes?

But ah ! we weep, that he from us fhould
  part,

Who fo minutely trac'd the finner's heart;

Who all the reafonings therein difclos'd,
And all the Devil's ftratagems expos'd ;
The man whom God firft raifed (in his
     youth)
In WALES, to propogate the Gofpel truth,
He fet his brow as brafs, no flefh he fear'd,
Effential truth he faithfully declar'd.
His grace, and knowledge, numbers to him
     drew,
They to his houfe, like doves to windows, flew,
Thoufands he caus'd, by the great pow'r of
     God,
To part with fin, and fly to JESU's blood.
He fpake nor did his works his words deny,
He liv'd each day, as tho' that day to die.
   O Moon, and Stars, who make the dark-
     nefs light,
Tell us how oft he groan'd to God by night.
Say, rifing Sun, yea tell us dawning day,
How foon he left his bed, to praife and pray.
                              Say

Say walls, and clofets, ev'ry fecret place,
How oft he fupplicated GOD for grace,
How oft he with his bleffed Lord did meet,
And fill'd with love, bow'd at his facred feet.
Say, thou infernal Prince, how thou didft
    rage,
When HARRIS did againft thy caufe engage;
And let thine emiffaries here proclaim,
That mov'd by thee, they vilify'd his name.
Say ye bleft Angels, how difpatch'd from
    GOD,
To guard him round on ev'ry fide ye ftood.
Say Sinners fay, how oft with warm defire,
He warn'd you to efcape eternal fire.
   Let towns, and ftreets, houfes, and fields
    proclaim,
His conftant ardour for his JESU's name.
Then let each Chriftian with a fecret figh,
Reverberate TREVECKA's penfive cry.

Let ev'ry heart lift up a fervent pray'r,

That old ELIJAH's mantle may be there.

That God from age, to age, may carry on,

Th' amazing work which HARRIS hath be-

gun.

That all who fhall that Saint of God fucceed,

Like him, may prove true Ifraelites indeed.

Not all the pow'rs of hell could him dif-

may,

He to the end purfu'd the narrow way.

The paths of peace inceffantly he trod,

Then dy'd exulting in his Saviour God.

His fpirit catholic was friend to all,

Who Jefu's image bore, and name did call,

A mighty conqu'ror as in life in death,

Cry'd vict'ry, vict'ry, to his lateft breath,

And tho' his body felt moft poignant fmart,

He faid " the dear Redeemer keeps my

heart,"

And

And when the great I AM fhall burn the
      fkies,
And bid unnumber'd Worlds to Judgment
      rife,
Then HARRIS by his Lord fhall be confeft,
And foul, and body, enter into reft,
Return triumphant to his deftin'd Throne,
And dwell with God, in extacies unknown.

On the Death of the Rev. Mr. WATKINS,
   of LANURSK, in the County of BRECON,
   who died the 9th of Jan. 1774.

Let me die the Death of the Righteous, and let my latter
End be like his.

ALAS! what mournful tidings ftrike my
      foul!
Ye Heav'nly Pow'rs, my paffions now con-
    troul,

       I 3   WATKINS

WATKINS is gone—is number'd with the
　　dead!
And all his loving partner's joys are fled !
Now all his words affectionate and kind,
And ev'ry look, is recent on her mind,
She views the token * of their mutual love,
And weeps there is no Father to reprove,
Who wisely rul'd with a paternal care,
And in her joys and griefs a part did bear,
Thus waves of grief acrofs her bosom roll,
And fill with deep diftrefs her penfive foul !

　　But she alone doth not fuftain the lofs,
For ev'ry lover of the Saviour's crofs,
With whom he did in Chriftian union meet,
The death of WATKINS greatly muft regret.
In him they loft a brother and a friend,
On whom for counfel fage they might de-
　　pend :
　　* A Child about fix years old.

　　　　　　　　　　　　　　　A

A kind reprover, but with all fincere,

Kind to the finner, to the fin fevere.

To fpeak effential truths he did not fhun,

Not partial to the great, ———

A faithful Monitor and Father he,

For gifts unequall'd in fociety ;

A public Lab'ror, zealous for his God,

Who pointed finners to the Saviour's Blood.

A bleffed inftrument thro' God hath been,

Of calling numbers from the paths of fin.

Belov'd of God, he did in God confide,

For " By his works his Faith was jufti-

     fy'd."

Each truly Chriftian grace in him was found ;

Oh ! cruel Death why didft thou give the

       wound,

Why didft thou not permit his ufeful days ;

Who only liv'd to found his Maker's praife ?

But

But ah ! 'tis nature speaks, let Faith arise
And view the Saint ascending to the skies;
His Lord for glory made his servant meet,
Then call'd him hence to worship at his feet,
Hark ! how the Heav'nly Choir began to
    sing,
A song of praise, when WATKINS enter'd in.
To see another of the Blood-bought race,
Return'd from sorrow, glory to embrace.
But oh ! what extacies his soul possess'd,
When he beheld the glories of the bless'd !
When he beh ld, without a vail betw een,
What once as through a glass was darkly
    seen !
His glorious Lord, in all his God-like
    charms !
And heard him, bid him welcome to his
    arms.
                    " Come

" Come my belov'd by purchafe thou art
           mine,
" Be Life, eternal Life for ever thine."
   Thus fares the Saint, who while he dwelt
          below,
A world of fin and pain and grief did know,
Now he beholds among the ranfom'd few,
Thofe whom he lately in the body knew,
Who juft before him gain'd the happy fhore,
With joy they meet their Jefus to adore.
No noneffentials there the Saints difpute,
Nor will they wifh each other to confute,
Their only ftrife, who loudeft fhall proclaim
The matchlefs glory of the flaughter'd Lamb
Who has redeem'd us by his precious Blood
And made us Kings, and Priefts, and fons of
       God.‡
   Children of God, who now the body wear,
Are not your hearts now panting to be there?
          ‡ Rev. i, 5, 6.   Are

Are not your very inmoſt ſouls on fire,

Thus to be chanting with the heav'nly choir?

Your ſpirit thus releaſ'd and ſoar away,

To dwell with WATKINS in eternal day.

Who would not like our lov'd EUSEBIUS die

Who when he found his diſſolution nigh,

More than a conqu'ror thro' his Saviour's
       Blood,

Could ſay " my life is hid with CHRIST in
       GOD !"

Commending all to JESU's ſpecial grace,

He ſweetly bow'd his dying head in peace.

  Oh ! why ſhould we the death of Saints
       deplore

And mourn as tho' they dy'd to live no
       more ?

Henceforth forbear to weep, but ſtrive to
       raiſe

Our feeble pow'rs in GOD our Saviour's
       praiſe.   But

But tho' each Chriftian's heart might well
      rejoice,

When thus by death they hear their fover-
      eign's voice,

Let carelefs finners aliens from their GOD,

Who never knew the worth of JESU's Blood,

With horror tremble, when in tender love

They hear the Saviour call his Saints above :

For when the laft * elect is gather'd in

Adieu ! to all the advocates for fin,

Adieu ! to ev'ry pleafure, fport, and game,

Except they find them in the gen'ral flame,

Then thofe who oft' the good have vilify'd,

Shall be by GOD eternally deny'd.

When WATKINS in the number of the juft,

Shall find admittance, with a " Come ye
      bleft,"

" Enter the Kingdom, I prepar'd for you

" Ere earth or fea their firft exiftence knew.

              Math. xx, iv. 31.

                             On

On the Death of the Author's Mother,
Mrs. CAVE, of BRECON, who died
Feb. 6, 1777.

And I heard a voice from Heaven, saying unto me, Write,
Blessed are the Dead which die in the Lord, from
henceforth: Yea, saith the Spirit, that they may rest
from their Labours; and their works do follow them.
REV. xiv. 13.

'TIS done,—'tis GOD has call'd her—I
    submit,
And humbly own that best which he thinks
    fit.
But ah! when first I heard the direful news,
My wounded soul all comfort did refuse,
I heard—I felt---I funk beneath the stroke,
With very grief my vital spirits broke.
I view'd the dear lov'd face, consign'd to
    death,
                    And

And heard her blefs me with her parting
     breath.
My heart was full, and in my grief I cry'd,
Oh! that I had with my dear Mother dy'd;
A thoufand of her foft endearing words
Flew to my mind, and pierc'd my heart like
     fwords.
She gave me birth, and more than twenty
     years,
I've been the object of her anxious cares.
Through helplefs infancy fhe fav'd from
     harms,
And nurs'd, and bore me in her tender arms.
She fympathiz'd in all my pain and grief,
And would have borne it all for my relief.
   And is that precious life for ever o'er?
And fhall I know maternal love no more?
In vain this vaft terreftrial ball I trace,
I view no more that lovely, deareft face:
No more her tender, Chriftian letters fee,
Nor hear how oft fhe wept, and pray'd for me.

O worſt of days, that has bereft of life,

So dear a Mother, and ſo lov'd a Wife.

Where ſhall I go to eaſe my burthen'd heart?

Where find a friend, who'll with me bear a
      part?

Alas! there's none—O let me weep and ſigh!

I'll mourn, and wail my loſs until I die!

    Thus Nature felt, and ſpoke; for Reaſon
      fled,

And Faith, and Hope, lay bury'd with the
      dead;

But there's a GOD, a never-failing friend,

Whoſe pity, love, and goodneſs know no end.

I knew him ſuch, I to his footſtool flew,

And found his promiſes were firm and true.

He heard my ſad complaint, he gave relief,

And bade me riſe ſuperior to my grief.

Huſh—Nature—then I cry'd, nor more
      complain,

She only left a world of grief and pain,

                   To

To enter manfions of eternal reft,

To live, and reign with GOD for ever bleft.

How patient in affliction, how refign'd,

How meet for glory was her peaceful mind!

She welcom'd Death, and faid, *L O R D,*
        quickly come;

And take me hence, I long to be at home.

She bleft her houfe, and bid them ceafe to
        weep,

Then, with a fmile, in CHRIST, fhe fell
        afleep.

    Hail then, dear Saint, in thy immortal joy!

In blifs fuperlative, without alloy.

Live with thy GOD, nor let my partial mind

E'er wifh thy ftay from joys fo unconfin'd;

But let my grateful heart in praife afcend

To that all-gracious, all-victorious friend,

Who guided, lov'd, and kept thee to the
        end.

K 2   EPITAPHS.

EPITAPHS.

On a YOUNG MAN, who died Three Days
after he was married.

ALL flesh is grafs—Important truth!
Nor dare we boaft of health or youth,
The nuptial bed I fcarce had trod,
Ere fummon'd forth to meet my GOD,
Compell'd to leave my weeping Bride,
Sunk from her tender arms, and dy'd.

Another

Another, On a YOUNG LADY.

BEHOLD ye thoughtlefs young and gay,
    What I am now, ye fhortly may.
I preach whilft here I mould'ring lie,
And this my text—*Prepare to die!*

Another, On an AMIABLE WIFE.

SHE's gone !—The dear companion of
        my bed,
And with her ev'ry earthly blifs is fled ;
An empty world is all I now can boaft,
With her my ev'ry wifh and joy was loft.

K 3   POEMS

P O E M S

ON RELIGIOUS SUBJECTS.

On hearing the Rev. Mr. R————D read
the Morning Service, and preach in
ST. THOMAS's Church, WINCHESTER.

WHEN plac'd within the confecrated
       Ifle,
In penfive folitude I fat awhile;
At length with all the grace that Heav'n in-
      fpires,
All that folemnity the Church requires,

Began

Began the facred order of the day :
The Reverend R———d did each truth
    convey,
With fuch an emphafis as muft impart
A facred pleafure to each pious heart,
With fuch a cadence he difmifs'd each claufe,
As fhou'd enforce a GOD's eternal laws.

    Not as fome Priefts, who run o'er ev'ry
    pray'r,
As tho' no truth, or foul, or GOD were there.
The giddy hearer enters gay and vain,
And unaffected leaves the Church again ;
While leffer truths deliver'd on the ftage,
Or even fictions, will each mind engage,
Becaufe the player labours through his part,
To claim attention, and affect the heart.

    If in a tragic character he moves,
And treats of deaths, or difappointed loves,
                    Then

Then all the horrors confequent on death,
Dart from his eyes, and fpeak in ev'ry breath.
Does he th' afflicted lover perfonate,
Then all that fofter paffion can create,
Solicitude—love—anguifh—grief—defpair,
Yea ev'ry figh, and languid look is there,
'Till each fpectator's eyes with tears o'erflow,
And thus concludes this fcene of fancy'd woe.
 But truth's eternal, facred, and divine,
Where goodnefs, majefty, and juftice fhine;
Yea truths on which our future hopes de-
   pend,
Truths which the moft exalted mind tran-
   fcend;
That awful tragedy in which a GOD
Pray'd, agoniz'd, and bath'd the ground
   with blood;
That tragedy from which the Sun withdrew,
Nor wou'd his crucifying Maker view;
       That

That love,—ftupendous · love,—furpaffing
  thought,
Which paid our ranfom, tho' fo dearly
  bought.
Thefe truths fublime the audience coldly
  hear,
Nor ever deign to drop a feeling tear;
While at the play each bofom heaves a figh,
Lo ! in the Church unmov'd they fit,—But
  why ?
The Prieft to whom the Embaffy is giv'n,
Who is the high Ambaffador of Heav'n,
Treats facred truth with cold indifference,
As tho' 'twere fiction, or impertinence.
Celeftial themes, that move a Seraph's lyre,
Droop on his tongue, and on his lips expire;
While the wife Actor aims by his addrefs,
Each fiction as undoubted truth t'imprefs.
      Would

Would thofe Divines, whom love canno
    induce,
Whofe languid hearts no ardor can diffufe,
(Whofe feet, perhaps, the church wou'd
    ne'er frequent,
If not infpir'd by her emolument),
Would even gain inftruction from the ftage,
By any means their audience to engage.
Left months and years fhould run their am-
    ple round,
And when the Mafter comes, no fruit be
    found.
No prodigal brought home, no fin fubdu'd,
No Saint advanc'd in grace, nor mind re-
    new'd.
All's barren ground, when an incenfed God,
Will from the Prieft require his people's
    blood.

An

An HYMN in Time of OPPOSITION.

O LORD a poor defpifed few,
    Once more together meet ;
Diftill on each thy heav'nly dew,
    And lay us at thy feet.

May each as the elect of GOD,
    Bowels of mercy know ;
And as the purchafe of thy blood,
    In all thy foot-fteps go.

Give us thy fpirit, gentle, mild,
    To teach us, Lord, that when
We are like thee, by man revil'd,
    Not to revile again.

And if we fuffer for thy caufe,
    O let us not repine,

                                        But

But simply talk, and bear thy Crofs,
   And prove that we are thine.

Let no oppofing fpirit reign,
   But let us, through thy grace,
From all religious wars refrain,
   And follow after peace.

Thus let us by our works of love,
   Conftrain our foes to fay,
" We only feek our home above,
   And tread the narrow way."

Another Hymn.

COME thou all prevailing Spirit,
   Come and teach me how to pray,
Intercede for Jesu's merit,
   Wafh and take my fins away.

              How

How much need of that attonement,
  Hath a guilty foul like me ?
Who am not one fleeting moment,
  From fome fimple paffion free.

Sin, where e'er I go, I find it,
  Find it woven in my heart;
To thy crofs, O Jefus ! bind it,
  Sin deftroy, and grace impart:
Sin, like weeds, for ever fpringing,
  Doth the foil throughout defile ;
All my life's a life of finning,
  Oh ! I'm viler than the vile

Yes, I fin in ev'ry action,
  Sin in ev'ry word and thought ;
I can't pray without diftraction,
  Sin, on all I do is wrote.
When I to my clofet enter,
  Seeking peace, in JESU's blood,

L   Swift,

Swift, as thought, intrudes the Tempter,
   Drives, or draws, my heart from God.

Thus while I am proftrate lying,
   While my lips, in prayer move,
While, with feeming ardour crying,
   For redemption, from above;
Lo! I find, at that dread inftant,
   My vain heart is rov'd away,
Wander'd off, on fomething diftant,
   And my lips alone do pray.

Then abafh'd, I filent wonder,
   Why is fuch a rebel fpar'd?
Why not caft amongft that number,
   In eternal chains referv'd?
Then with fhame and joy confounded,
   I exult in fovereign grace,
Grace which hath to me abounded,
   Me, the worft of ADAM's race.

                        Lord,

Lord, if I forget to praife thee,
  Let my tongue forget to move;
Jesu, 'to thy likenefs raife me,
  Let me all thy goodnefs prove;
Let my guilt be now abfolved,
  My whole nature fanctify,
Lord, I long to be diffolved,
  Make me meet, and let me die.

On the Firft General Fast after the
  Commencement of the late War.

WHEN direful judgments pour in like
      flood,
And fields, alas! are drench'd with human
      blood,
When armies after armies proftrate lie,
And brother, by his brother's hand muft die,
                    L 2   When

When kingdoms feem to rife, or empires
 fall,
One great Omnipotent conducts it all,
And thofe have but a fuperficial fcan,
Who view no higher origin than Man.

 Be ftill, methinks I hear JEHOVAH cry,
Be ftill before your GOD, and know 'tis I!
'Tis I make peace, and I create ftern war,
And ride to battle in my flaming car,
I guide the bullet, point the glitt'ring fword,
Defeat, or conqueft, wait my awful word.
But do I pleafure in deftruction take,
Or have your fins not bid the fword awake?
Do not a nation's fad offences call
For national calamities to fall?

 Great Sov'reign Lord, we own thy judgments juft,
And hide our guilty faces in the duft;

     Rejoice

Rejoice to hear a day is fanctify'd
T' implore thy aid, and humble BRITAIN's
    pride.
But may we not in this incur the rod, .
And make a folemn mockery of GOD?
T'abftain from food, to take our prayer-
    books,
And walk to Church with evangelic looks;
To bend the knee, or move the lips in
    pray'r,
If all the heart be not engaged there,
Is empty fhew, a poor external part,
While GOD, the Omnifcient GOD, demands
    the heart;
And fhould we fail in this grand facrifice,
The whole will be offenfive in his eyes.

    Defcend, celeftial dove, with holy fire,
And pure devotion ev'ry foul infpire.

                      Let

May vital pray'r, exprefs'd by ardent fighs,
Afcend to GOD, and penetrate the fkies.
Let all the nation thus with fafting turn,
And heart fincere, their paft tranfgreffions
          mourn;
Then is eternal truth engag'd to blefs,
And crown our juft petitions with fuccefs.

The Author being requefted on a Sunday
   Evening, by a Company of gay Ladies, to
   write a few Lines of POETRY inftantane-
   oufly, fhe accordingly prefented them
   with the following.

WHEN you, good Ladies, bid me write,
      My drowfy Mufe had took her flight,
But ere fhe reach'd her moffy bed,
I gave a call, and back fhe fled.

I humbly afk'd her what to fay,
She anfwer'd—" On a fabbath day,
" If you prefume to write a line,
" Be careful that it is divine,
" For know that ev'ry word and thought
" Shall be to ftricteft judgment brought,
" And what is now tranfacted here,
" Shall to unnumber'd worlds appear;
" When Earth fhall from her center fly,
" And ftars defert the blazing fky,
" When frighted fouls in vain fhall call
" For rocks and hills on them to fall.
" Then let this day and night be fpent,
" As in that day you'll not repent."

On

A Poem, occafioned by hearing prophane
Curfing and Swearing.

AND can we wonder, if the fword
    Is plung'd in Brothers blood?
If threat'ning vengeance flies around
    From a tremendous God.

When daring finners thus prefume
    His anger to provoke,
When daily with impunity
    His dread command is broke.

What hath eternal truth declar'd,
    None guiltlefs fhall remain,
Who fwears by ought in Heav'n or Earth,
    Or takes his name in vain.

Yet imprecations fill our ftreets,
    And bold blafphemers dare
                      Invoke

Invoke damnation from above,
   And by JEHOVAH fwear.

Their impious breath pollutes the air,
   Omnipotence defies,
Compels a long forbearing GOD,
   In judgment to arife.

What ! trifle with that facred name,
   Whofe goodnefs gives us breath !
Or Juftice fmites our feeble frame,
   And chains us down in Death.

Will not incenfed Majefty
   In vengeance lift his hand,
And bid deferved judgments fall
   On fuch a guilty land.

O when will finners ceafe from fin,
   And call for bleffings down ?
Then fhall the fword be fheath'd again,
   And laurels deck the crown.

On the Departure of Six Miffionaries to
    America, foon after the Death of the
    Rev. Mr. W.

WHEN once the foul, arifing from the
       dead,
Drinks the new wine, and eats the living
       bread,
It thirfts, it pants, it prays, for all to tafte
This heav'nly banquet, this celeftial feaft.
The bleft ambition this, the pray'r of thefe,
Who brave the dangers of the boift'rous
       feas.

   Go heralds, go! and may the God of
       peace
Go with you—guide you—ftrengthen you
       with grace.

                   Lo!

Lo ! we commend you to his fpecial care !

Go forth in confidence, your Lord is near.

Nor rocks, nor feas, nor raging billows
    dread,

His potent fhield fhall fcreen each favour'd
    head.

Think how the winds and feas his voice
    obey'd

Your fov'reign Lord ! be not by ought dif-
    may'd;

And whilft on board, may JESUS be your
    guide,

In calmeft feas, and o'er the rougheft tide.

So fhall each foul 'crofs the broad deep fur-
    vive,

Till at the port defir'd ye all arrive.

There, like young champions from great
    W———— fprung,

Fly round, and gain for CHRIST a num'rous
    throng !

                W————

W——— called thoufands, JESUS to adore!

But may you call ten thoufand thoufands
    more!

Go forth like DAVID, with your fling and
    ftone,

And bear the world, and fin, and SATAN
    down,

Fight on courageous for your Saviour GOD,

Nor e'er recoil—atteft the truth to blood.

Stand firm, (nor fear the men, or Devils
    frown,

Endure the Crofs, and wear the Heav'nly
    Crown.

O bleft Americans, how well might ye

Exult with utmoft joy, whilft penfive we

Sit forrowing here, and each to each deplore

Our abfent friends perhaps to meet no more.

O bleffed GOD! do thou our grief fuftain,

And let us know we have not heard in vain.

                                        Their

Their faithful exhortations bring to mind,
And teach us to revere thefe left behind.
And when this tranfitory life is paft,
O may we meet around thy throne at laft.
There, fill'd with love, our gracious God
       adore,
. And weep, and figh, and part with friends
    no more!

On hearing the TOLLING of a BELL, in a
very unhealthy Spring, when great Numbers were carried off.

WHAT do I hear—or fancy that I
        hear?
(As long accuftom'd to the doleful found)
The tolling of yon melancholy bell!
Which has for weeks and months inceffantly

Some dreadful ftory in my ears proclaim'd,
And with repeated ftrokes alarm'd the town !
 Alas ! 'tis more than fancy——Hark it
   ftrikes !
Yea, more in language moft emphatical
It fpeaks—My inmoft foul with horror fills.
What does the dread but true informer fay?
What doth it intimate or what declare ?
Not that fome valiant chief, mighty in
   arms,
Returns, with honour and with conqueft
  crown'd :
Nor that a noble heir is lately born,
Whofe birth makes joyful his glad parents
  hearts,
And proves perhaps a blifs to future days :
Nor that the nuptial knot has juft been ty'd
Between fome happy pair, who mutually
Agree, to fpend their future days in love's
       Em-

Embrace—Nor is it what wou'd be lefs
       pleafing,
That fome intolerable woe is near,
If an expedient be not quickly found
T'avert, or diffipate th' impending ftroke ;
For were it thus, each may allay his grief,
And with a peradventure quell the figh.
But ah ! it leaves us not one glimpfe of hope,
More than portention in its voice is heard.
It tells us that the fatal dart is fled,
Lodg'd in the vitals, in the heart, or
       head,
Of fome one of the race of fallen Adam :
And that an aweful feparation's made,
The fpirit forc'd from her clay tenement,
Prepar'd, or unprepar'd, away fhe's fled,
To ftand before the heart, rein-trying GOD.
And now her die eternally is caft
In fad perdition, or in endlefs blifs.

In

In vain ten thoufand arts would now com-
      bine,

Ten thoufand briny fhow'rs be pour'd in
      vain,

Or all the treafures of the Indies brought,

To make the foul refume her wonted feat,

Or actuate th' inanimated clay.

Such is the conqueft, fuch the pow'r of
      death,

Who daily fome new trophy doth erect,

To fhew how univerfally he reigns.

O thou inimitable King of Terrors !

Shall none efcape from thy vexatious jaws,

But wilt thou ftill continue to deftroy,

Nor heed what age, what quality, or fex ?

The tender babe, the great, the wife, the
      good,

The hoary head, the mean, the weak, the
      vile,

                        Are

Are all by thee, alike, reduc'd to duft !
Deftruction is effential to thy nature,
And formidable is thy very name.

But oh ! my foul why rageft thou at death ?
He is but the vicegerent of his GoD.
Nor did he ever give the mortal wound,
Until the fatal mandate had been feal'd,
And fent from the tremendous court of
      Heav'n :
And then, indeed, obfequious to his GoD,
And deaf to all the cries of finful man,
At once he executes the dread command.
'Tis Heav'ns decree, fince thy firft parents
      finn'd,
(And doft thou at the juft decree repine ?)
That ev'ry foul of man fhould pafs thro'
      death.
So, if thou traceft matters to their fource,
That monfter Sin was the efficient caufe

Of

Of all calamities, of ev'ry death.;

Of that for which I now hear yonder knell,

Which brings this fecret horror o'er my
    heart.

  Sinner awake, the deathly fignal hear, .·

Regard it as a monitor to thee !

A gracious call, a fpecial voice from Heav'n !

But ah ! Death's vifits now fo frequent are ;

Men laugh at Death, and lightly of him
    deem !

Tho' dead in fin, and enemies to GoD,

They think to meet him with an air of
    triumph ;

Nor ever dream, that, at his dread approach,

Ten thoufand horrors will at once awake !

Confcience, tho' ftifled till that very moment,

Will like fome potent prince victorious rife,

And act the part for which it was defign'd.

Open the book of records, and arrange

                    In

In dread array* before the finner's mind,
Ten thoufand times ten thoufand paft tranf-
     greffions !
Which had for years as in oblivion laid,
(Then blacken'd with the thought of flighted
     grace,)
Will all appear—diftract the guilty mind,
And drive the frantic foul to deep defpair.

   Then with a fearful looking for of death,
She dies—and finks into the dark abyfs,
Nor ever knows a period to her pains.
For ftill, and ftill, and ftill, 'tis " wrath to
     come !"
O then vain man, " work while 'tis call'd
     to-day,"
Bethink thyfelf, before it be too late,
Fall quickly to foliloquy, and fay——
Am I not mortal, like my fellow-creatures ?

   * A law term, as well as military.

                   And

And can I call one inch of time my own,
Or boaſt myſelf in the approaching hour ?
With great celerity my moments fly,
Surely my days will ſhortly find a period !

    Suppoſe it now !—Bring Death's pale aſ-
          pect near,
See him and his concomitants advance !
Fancy the well aim'd arrow on the wing,—
Sev'ring thy ſoul from all terreſtrial things !
To ſtand before the great tremendous Judge,
Whoſe piercing eye hath taken cognizance
Of ev'ry thought, and word, and act, unjuſt,
By thee committed, but by thee forgot !
Lo ! the minuteſt has not miſs'd his notice,
Nor ſlipt the mind of the eternal all.

    How ſtands thy ſoul affected at the
        thought ?
Ah ! is there not a ſomething that recoils

                    And

And wifhes to poftpone the fatal hour ?

This argues all is not aright within :

And that if death fhould find thee as thou
    art.

Thou wouldft not die, as doth a bird, or
    beaft,

Who are annihilated at their death,

But dying, die, and die, and never die.

O then redeem thy time, to JESUS fly,

With fpeed take fhelter in his bleeding
    wounds,

Who only takes away Death's poignant fting

And turns the ghaftly monfter to a friend.

Make fure thy int'reft in the bleeding lamb,

Nor let him reft, until he fpeaks thee peace,

Then come whatever may, come life or
    death,

To live will then be CHRIST, to die be gain.

Death will be more defir'd by thy foul,

                Than

Than all the honours that the world beſtows:
For by his friendly hand thou'lt part with ſin,
And from a world of ſorrow, grief, and pain,
To the immediate preſence of thy GOD.
There baſk in ſeas of uncreated bliſs!
In extacies to worms on earth unknown!
With Angels and Arch-angels, ſweetly join,
To ſing the praiſes of a Triune GOD.

An HYMN for CONSECRATION, ſung
at the Opening of the Counteſs of *Hun-*
tingdon's Chapels in *Brecon*, *Worceſter*, &c.

COME JESUS! come, and bleſs this place!
        'Tis open'd in thy name;
Deſcend with ſhow'rs of heav'nly grace,
        And conſecrate the ſame.

Eternal God, our pray'r attend,
　　Diffuse thy love around :
As to the burning-bush, descend,
　　And make it holy ground !

Bid each the man of sin put by !
　　As Moses did of old
His shoes put off, when he drew nigh,
　　Thy glory to behold.

Lord, let thy glory fill this place,
　　Yea fill each sinner's heart :
Come thou incarnate Prince of Peace,
　　And never more depart.

In vain we are assembl'd here,
　　If Jesus does not come :
Appear, thou bleeding Lamb, appear,
　　Let ev'ry heart make room !

　　　　　　　　　　Within

Within thefe walls let thoufands, Lord,
　　Thro' grace be born of thee ;
And in this place thy name record
　　'Till time no more fhall be.

Now, Saviour, now thy work begin,
　　Thy potent arm difplay :
Let fome poor rebel dead in fin
　　Be made alive to-day !

Call fome poor wand'rer by thy grace,
　　Who knew thee not before :
So fhall we blefs thee for this place
　　When time fhall be no more.

An HYMN for CHRISTMAS.

AWAKE each heart, rejoice and fing,
　　Salute the morn that CHRIST our King,
　　　　Affumes

Affumes our flefh and blood;
Sinners, 'twas life for you and me,
When CHRIST partook our mifery,
All hail the Saviour GOD!

IMMANUEL is the Saviour's name,
Yes GOD with us, O glorious theme!
Shout, fhout the news abroad,
With fpeed the wond'rous tidings tell,
A GOD defcends with Man to dwell!
All hail the babe, the GOD!

The great I AM, who all things made,
The world's ftupendous pillars laid;
Earth trembles at his nod:
Him whom eternal ages crown'd,
Is as an helplefs infant found:
All hail the Saviour GOD!

N

O

O wond'rous! O amazing love!
Which brought the Saviour from above;
    'Twas he the vine prefs trod!
His church's fins on him were laid,
And he the mighty debt hath paid:
    All hail the babe, the GOD!

Bid Satan, felf, and fin depart,
Bid JESUS welcome to your heart,
    He bore your wond'rous load;
In him the father's reconcil'd,
Well pleas'd alone in Mary's child,
    All hail the Saviour GOD!

In grateful fongs your voices raife,
From fea, to fea, refound his praife,
    Give, give the Saviour laud;
All Heav'n aftonifh'd ftands, that he
Should deign the fon of man to be,
    To make us fons of GOD.

                      On

On the GENERAL FAST,

February 8, 1782.

OMNIPOTENT eternal all,
 By whom ftates rife or empires fall,
Whofe potent word creates a world,
Or bids it be to atoms hurl'd.

Lord of all Lords, and King of Kings,
Beginning, center, end of things;
Fountain of light, of life, and love,
Through worlds below, and worlds above.

Wond'rous I AM, myfterious word,
Who canft, or draw, or fheath the fword.
We reptiles, who of duft are made,
Prefume to fupplicate thy aid.

To

To thee we dedicate this day,
To mourn for fin, to faft and pray!
Thy wond'rous works of old declare
The great effects of fervent pray'r.

Does Mofes but in fpirit groan,
Lo! it prevails before thy throne.
The boift'rous waves at once divide,
And form a wall on either fide.

Again he lifteth up his hands,
Ifrael a conqu'ring army ftands :
But when his fervent fpirit fails,
They fall, and Amaleck prevails.

The Ninevites its influence knew,
And jointly to thy footftool flew :
They mourn, they faft, to Heav'n they cry,
And turn th' impending judgment by.

                                    May

May we like them confefs our fin,
The renovating work begin,
Timely avert thy vengeful rod,
And Jacob-like prevail with GOD!

Our land, our finking land protect,
Our king and fenators direct;
Our fleets preferve, our armies blefs,
And bid the nation fhout fuccefs.

Our foes, our envious foes annoy,
And all their impious plots deftroy.
Let peace her wifh'd for banner fpread,
And laurels deck our fov'reign's head.

On

On hearing the Rev. Mr. B—— from
PSALM 65, 2.

O thou that heareſt Prayer, unto thee ſhall all fleſh come.

WITH calm attention lo! I heard,
My heart the ſage divine rever'd,
While he with holy zeal explain'd
The gracious words his text contain'd.
I'll bid the muſe the theme prolong,
And form the ſubſtance in a ſong.

To GOD the Lord ſhall man repair
By public and by private pray'r;
Thus humbly his dependance own
On thee, thou infinite, unknown.
Where two or three are met in pray'r,
Lo! GOD has promis'd to be there;

He's

He's there a prefent help to blefs,
Crown each petition with fuccefs,
Or in his wifer way our wants redrefs.

    If warm'd by pure devotion's fire,
We to our clofet fhould retire,
There, unperceiv'd by human eye,
Pour forth to GOD our plaintive cry,
Or fend before the throne a contrite figh,
Lo! he'll on wings of love defcend,
And to our various wants attend.
Here we may get our hearts renew'd,
And each unruly luft fubdu'd :
Here virtue draw from JESU's blood,
And hold fweet intercourfe with GOD :
Here we may all our griefs reveal,
Nor one beloved fin conceal ;
For, e'er we fpeak, Omnifcience knows
What all our words and tears difclofe ;

                      Then

Then fome celeftial cordial gives,
And lo! the contrite finner lives.

    Not all the wealth the Indies own,
Crowns or the moft exalted throne,
Shou'd counterpoife the blifs of pray'r,
When God is by his prefence there.
In pray'r feraphic joys we find,
Which quite transform the earthly mind.
The man who always, ere he pray'd,
From the bright path of duty ftray'd,
Lo! now he gladly runs therein,
And hates the garments ftain'd by fin. ·

    This change is in himfelf alone,
For changes are to God unknown,
(Fixt as his own eternal name)
To-day and yefterday's the fame :
With endlefs glory to reward
Each humble follower of the Lord;

                    And

And fixt his purpofe to difdain
The foul who will in fin remain,
Who flights the offers of his grace,
And never bows to feek his face.

As foon may man by air exift,
Or brutes without their food fubfift;
The feather'd warblers live in floods,
Or the finn'd tribes amid the woods;
As foon may Satan burn with love,
Or GOD a fount of envy prove,
As fhall the foul to heav'n afcend,
Who without pray'r his days fhall end.

When man has mifimprov'd his time,
And fpent his youth, and health, and
  prime,
Only his GOD to difobey,
When Death advances, he may pray,
But then his pray'r may be in vain,
'GOD juftly may his fuit difdain;

     He

He may, 'tis true, his grace extend,
And ev'n in death commence his friend:
So let the dying not defpair,
But oh! let all the living fear;
For on an awful chance depends
A world of blifs that never ends.
GOD may accept—and he may not—
He may thy name for ever blot
Out of his book of life divine,
And thy fad foul to Hell confign.

Then form your hearts in health to pray,
Nor let appearances difmay
Your feeking fouls :—Tho' good men lie
On beds of languifhment, and die,
And tho' the wicked feem to rife
On tow'ring pinions to the fkies,
Think not the juft has no reward,
Or is forgotten by his Lord,

Or

Or that his wrath does not remain
On thofe who do his grace difdain:
The wicked lives but to fulfil
The direful meafure of his ill;
Each day ftill makes the finner worfe,
And life by fin becomes a curfe;
The greater his iniquity,
The more his punifhment will be.
The good man dies, leaves earth and pain,
A crown of glory to obtain;
And if thro' life God try'd his grace,
'Twas but his glory to increafe.

Let man before his GOD be ftill,
Pray with fubmiffion to his will:
If what we afk be for our good,
'Twill not be by our Lord withftood;
But if he e'er our fuit denies,
'Twas wrong—for he's immenfely wife.

Nature

Nature wou'd aſk for health and reſt,

When pain and ſickneſs may be beſt,

Our droſſy nature to refine ;—

If ſo, be pain and ſickneſs mine.

The chaſt'ning rod I'll ne'er deſpiſe,

'Tis a rich bleſſing in diſguiſe.

   Be thus reſign'd and paſſive found,

In works of holineſs abound.

Let ev'ry word, and work, and thought,

Be into ſtrict obedience brought ;

But here beware of a miſtake,

Leſt that be fatal which you make.

Think not by this thy Heav'n to gain,

Or all thy righteouſneſs is vain ;

Nought but a Saviour's precious blood

Can give thy ſoul acceſs to GoD ;

Nought but his ſpotleſs righteouſneſs,

  (And not thy works) muſt be thy dreſs.

'Twas

'Twas he that firſt thy ſoul inſpir'd,
Thy heart with pure devotion fir'd;
He gave thee faith, and faith's increaſe, ⎫
Purchas'd thy pardon, ſeal'd thy peace, ⎬
And bid thee live and grow in grace. ⎭
He is the firſt, and he alone
The laſt, the great, and corner ſtone;
Who builds upon this rock ſhall ſtand,
Who builds without it, builds on ſand,
And be his fabrick ne'er ſo tall,
'Twill in the day of trial fall.

   Then wou'd you live and learn to die,
Live holy, yet your works decry;
And only hope a ſeat above,
Thro' boundleſs grace and dying love.

IN·

INGRATITUDE.

INGRATITUDE—thou fin accurft,
  Of ev'ry fin pronounc'd the worft;
Detefted weed, where e'er thou'rt found
Infernal poifon fwells the ground.

Chriftians, who at perfection aim,
Or to its facred heights attain,
God-like in all they act or fay,
Injuries with kindneffes repay.

Heathens, who led by nature's rays,
Nor ever bleft with gofpel days,
By nature's dictates underftood,
'Twere juft to render good for good.

Brutes, that of reafon ne'er poffeft,
Can act no higher than a beaft,
Led by their own revengeful will,
Will doubtlefs render ill for ill.

                                    But

But thou accurft, where e'er thou art,
Confcience will know and point the dart :
Thou who repayeft *good* with *evil*,
Art only equall'd by the Devil.

An HYMN for a CHILD who has loft its
FATHER or MOTHER.

O Thou who once didft children blefs,
 And take them in thy arms,
Defend the infant fatherlefs,
And guard my feet from harms.

Thou canft the lofs of friends fupply,
 And turn to good each ill;
Tho' ev'ry friend fhould fail or die,
 Thou art all gracious ftill.

O 2   Thy

Thy wifdom and thy pow'r I own,
   For all thy ways are juft;
The prince thou raifeft to his throne,
   Or lay'ft him down in duft.

May I obey thy facred word
   In thefe my infant days;
Grow up in all things like my Lord,
   And learn to lifp his praife.

So fhall I find thy promis'd reft,
   When this frail life is o'er,
And meet in my dear Saviour's breaft
   My friends fled hence before.

LOVE,

L O V E,

The ESSENCE of RELIGION.

NOT every one who crieth Lord,
   Or hear, or pray, or preach thy word,
Wilt thou in God-like accents own,
Or hail as partners of thy throne.

What if this sect or that I join,
Believe my party moſt divine,
Vain will my warmeſt notions prove,
If abſent from my heart, thy love.

What if with Calvin I agree,
Or to Arminian doctrines flee,
I ſtill remain a child of ſin,
If love does not preſide within.

Let

Let bigots for the fhell contend,
In idle controverfies fpend
Their precious time, who zealots fire
And notions (not thy love) infpire.

With me let names and parties fall,
Thy love, my fov'reign God, my all ;
The fubftance this :—Of this pöffeft,
'Mid flaming worlds I ftand confeft.

F I N I S.